JOURNEY TO PARADISE

Hilary Wilde

CHIVERS

British Library Cataloguing in Publication Data available

This Large Print edition published by BBC Audiobooks Ltd, Bath, 2008.
Published by arrangement with the Author's Estate.

U.K. Hardcover ISBN 978 1 408 41197 1
U.K. Softcover   ISBN 978 1 408 41198 8

Printed and bound in Great Britain by
CPI Antony Rowe, Chippenham, Wiltshire

CHAPTER ONE

Elaine Thomas was so angry that she could hardly speak as she looked at the liner's hostess, Fiona Kent.

'How can I dance with a man I've never met? We have to practise,' Elaine said. She was a tall, slender girl with graceful movements and a long cloud of fair hair and dark eyes that, now, were accusing. 'I thought Dirk Long, with whom I always dance, was to be my partner.'

'We thought so, too,' Fiona admitted. She was older than Elaine and already in her thirties, but she was an efficient hostess, attractive, friendly, sympathetic yet able to organise people into doing something they did not want to do. She also had fair hair, but hers was elaborately piled high and her long dark eyelashes looked, to Elaine, as if they might fall off at any moment. 'It is a shame,' Fiona went on, 'but you have to have a partner.'

A burst of music came down from one of the upper decks. The newly built liner, *Wonderland,* was about to start its first cruise. The passengers had been promised two weeks of sunshine, and if the weather let them down—for, after all, no one could control that!—Fiona's job was to see that the passengers enjoyed every moment of their

1

holiday at sea.

She sighed. 'I'd better go up and start meeting folk.'

'But look, let's settle this. Why isn't Dirk Long here? We understood that Dirk and I were engaged for the job.'

For a moment, Fiona looked amused. 'You seem very upset. You in love with him?'

Elaine blushed. She had often asked herself that question, for Dirk was fun, tall, handsome in a modern way, a fine dancer, but . . .

That one little word.

Then there was the actor, Mike West, who wanted her to try her luck on the stage. He, too, was good fun—at *times,* she had to admit. Maybe all men were difficult.

'In a way,' she answered Fiona's question. 'I nearly always dance with him. You can't just dance with anyone.'

'I'm afraid you have no choice.'

The deep voice startled them both and they turned their heads to look at the man standing in the open doorway of Fiona's small office. Elaine saw that he was tall, lean and blond before she noticed the sarcastic smile on his face that made something seem to slide down her spine. Why was he looking like that?

'After all,' the man added, 'it's just as difficult for me.'

Fiona stood up, her face eager and smiling. 'So it is you! I wasn't sure. She says she can't dance with a stranger.'

The man frowned, giving Elaine what she felt was a scathing up-and-down examination before he spoke. 'Are you sure,' he asked, 'that you shouldn't say: "I can't dance—full-stop"?'

'Of course I can dance,' Elaine said indignantly. 'Although I've worked as a secretary I've always done any exhibition dancing Mother has got booked. I can dance,' she added, defiantly.

'We'll soon see,' he said. 'I hope you're a good dancer, because this first voyage is important and we must keep the passengers happy.' He looked at his watch. 'Meet me in the Green Bar in an hour's time and we'll practise for tonight.' He left them, turning at the last moment to say with a smile: 'I'm afraid it's too late for you to prance off, Miss Thomas, because we're already on our way.' He closed the door as he spoke.

'Who is he?' Elaine asked. 'Of all the arrogant, impossible . . .!' She paused to draw in her breath. 'He really is the end!'

Fiona chuckled. 'Not many girls think that. He's on the Directors' Board and it means a lot to him that this first voyage should be a success.'

'But he's not a professional dancer,' Elaine almost wailed, imagining the horror of trying to dance before the passengers with a man who couldn't know what he was doing.

'He's a professional everything,' Fiona said, standing up. 'He's had a tough life and done

3

every job imaginable. His father died when he was young, then his mother was sick and he had a brother and two younger sisters he had to keep and educate. He's nice—when you know him.'

'I don't want to know him,' Elaine said crossly, and then wondered how she could *avoid* knowing him if they were to dance together as well as practising. What kind of dancer could he possibly be? Just an amateur, she thought scornfully.

An hour later she was to change her mind. She had spent the time on the upper decks, leaning over the rail, looking down at the crowd who were shouting farewells as the big white liner slowly drew away from the dock. The music pounded out and some of the passengers began to sing as well as laugh and chat. Elaine had looked round and seen that most of them were middle-aged or elderly married couples who, no doubt, were hoping to enjoy a really romantic holiday in the sunshine and one that had cost them surprisingly little. Then she had gone down to her cabin, far below in the centre of the liner, and had hastily unpacked. She was wearing a green trouser suit, as it was a cool autumn day, but now she hastily changed into a simple yellow dress which she usually wore when practising.

The Green Bar was on the top deck and closed, but her unwanted partner was waiting for her and took her inside. The floor was cleared of chairs and tables and there was a big record player.

The man gave her a long typed piece of paper. 'I've put down what dances we'll do each night. Incidentally, at five every afternoon—after tea—we give lessons to the passengers—just informally and *en masse,* which they seem to enjoy. However, if any of them want private lessons, they can be arranged to be given in here and . . .' He frowned. 'We don't charge anything—it's part of the cruise, but tell me first. You understand?'

Elaine was frowning a little as well as feeling surprised at the detailed information she was reading about the various dances they were to do—the Spanish fandango, waltzes, tangos. Every kind of dance, though most of them were out of date.

He seemed to read her thoughts. 'There are a lot of oldies among the passengers and they love the old dances. Let's get going,' he added as he put on a record. 'We shall start dancing with this one. Come on,' he added curtly as Elaine seemed to hesitate.

She went into his arms—stiffly. Not because she was nervous, but resentful, for had she known she was to dance with an unknown man—and such an unpleasant one, too!—she would never have taken the job and she was sure her mother would have understood. Two

5

dancers could quarrel like mad, could argue and fight, and end up by being bad dancers—that was where she and Dirk had always been successful, because they talked the same language in every way. But this man.

He danced well, but she felt her body resenting every moment and suddenly he stopped and grabbed her arms, giving her a good shake.

'Look,' he said angrily, 'stop this nonsense. No one made you take this job.'

She glared at him. 'I understood Dirk Long was to be my partner.'

'Did he tell you so?'

'No—no.' She hesitated, for he—this man—was right. Dirk had not said so, because he hadn't been there. 'He was away on holiday and . . . and I took it for granted my mother had arranged it with him.'

'She had—until the last moment.'

'He backed out?' she said slowly. It was so unlike Dirk, for this could have been great fun, at sea in the sunshine, doing the work they loved.

'Perhaps he'd been offered something more interesting,' the unpleasant man said with a smile. 'As it was the last minute, I had to step in. Believe me,' he went on bitterly, 'this is no pleasure, but the passengers must be amused. This is important. Now, listen to me.' His voice was growing quieter, yet somehow it sounded more threatening. 'Stop this stiff nonsense.

We're paying you good money and I expect to get good work for it. Relax and try to show me what sort of dancer you are, and if you're half as good as I was told you were. We haven't much time. We'll have to dance tonight. Come on.' His hand slid round her back and he held her hand tightly. 'Relax, I tell you,' he snapped.

He was right. She was being well paid. This was her job, so she tried to obey. At first it was difficult and everything she did was wrong. He spared her nothing: criticising, correcting and, worst thing of all, he was right each time and she was making the most stupid amateurish mistakes. He was a good dancer, she realised, as good as if not better than Dirk.

Gradually, as they tried different dances, she found her body relaxing, moving to the rhythm and beat of the music. Suddenly she found she was enjoying every moment of it— even the difficult following of his quick footsteps.

At last he stopped, switched off the record player and sat down, stretching out his long legs. She felt sorry it was finished—though at the same time she was glad it was over so she need not be with him much longer.

'Not bad at all,' he said, and although he sounded amused, the praise delighted her, surprising her because she was pleased at the same time. Why should she care what he thought of her? True, he was her employer—

she must remember that. Deep down inside her she felt hurt by Dirk's behaviour. True, they'd had a sort of quarrel just before he went on holiday, but he wasn't the kind to sulk or remember quarrels. 'What's your name? I've forgotten it,' the man sitting down by her side said abruptly.

'Elaine Thomas.'

'Of course. Elaine it is. We've got to have some details put up on the boards.'

'What's your name?' Elaine asked, then stopped, surprised at herself asking" him such a question and apparently surprising him even more.

'You mean to say you don't know?' He looked amused.

'If I did, would I ask?' she snapped.

He smiled, an amused sceptical smile. 'Well, I'm Garvin Humfrey and—' he began, then stopped as he saw the shocked, surprised look on Elaine's lovely face.

'You're . . . you're Garvin Humfrey?' she repeated slowly. 'But you can't be!' He was much too young. The Garvin Humfrey Tommy had told her about was an old man.

'And why can't I be?' he asked.

'I . . . I thought you were . . .' She paused, for there was no need to tell him that she knew his ward, Tommy Brenton—nor that she had thought Tommy's guardian could only be an old man, from his behaviour. Or that she was glad Tommy had thrown away his guardian's

8

cosseting and had run away to build up his own life, though he had left it rather late.

'You thought I was—what?' Garvin Humfrey asked with a smile.

She frowned, trying to find something to say that would not let him know she knew Tommy, and liked him and strongly disliked his guardian.

'I'd heard of you,' she said, which was the truth. 'And—and I thought you must be an old man.'

'Well, maybe I seem so to you. I'm thirty-one. How old are you? Nineteen?'

'Twenty-two.'

'You don't look it. I'd say you were very immature.'

It was all she could do to keep her mouth shut. She wanted to shout at him and tell him that *he* was the immature one. That Tommy needed a father-figure to help him—not that of a man who wanted to have nothing to do with him, except give him more money to make him shut up. Letting Tommy drift through life with no need to work, because he had a generous trust allowance, and as he said, he could always go to Uncle Garvin for help if he spent too much. There was no need for Tommy to work, so he didn't. He painted, and when she said to him that nobody could earn a living out of painting, he had told her the whole story. Why bother to work when he needn't? he had asked with that little-boy-lost smile.

Tommy was just twenty-three and about as immature as anyone could be, Elaine was thinking, as she looked at the tall, good-looking man who was staring at her thoughtfully. It was all *his* fault, Elaine was thinking, spoiling Tommy, encouraging him to be dependent and then giving him money and telling him to enjoy himself. What sort of life was that for a young man? Tommy had no ambition, not a desire to earn a penny. Wasn't it a bad thing to be given too much?

At least, her parents had taught her that! The treatment of children should be like that of birds who teach their babies to eat, to find food, look after themselves and then push them out of the nest, they said.

Elaine could remember her father saying that just before he died.

'That's what you should do with your kids, teach them to be independent but let them know you're there in times of emergency. Give them that feeling of security, and it's the greatest gift you can give your child.'

She had been treated like that. Getting a job as secretary as soon as she left school, and helping her mother in her dancing school in the evenings, having her own flat until her father died, yet always welcome at home. She had ambition, too, and was working hard for it. She wanted to be an exhibition dancer—to travel the world with Dirk by her side, listening to the wonderful sound of applause and cheers. That was why she had leapt at this job though it had been short notice and her boss hadn't been too pleased at her having two weeks' holiday soon after she had come back from her annual one.

'Well?' said Garvin Humfrey. 'Finished thinking?'

Elaine blushed, realising how long she had been silent. 'I'm sorry, I was thinking of my . . . my mother. Could I look at the dancing programme? We shall need a lot of practice.'

'Exactly. I suggest we have an hour before breakfast—if you can get up as early as that. Breakfast's at eight, so it means seven o'clock up here. Then we'll have another hour in the afternoon, after lunch when the bar is closed.' He handed her the long paper, so neatly typed.

She stared at it, interested, puzzled and then impressed.

'Who planned it all?'

Garvin Humfrey lit a cigarette and smiled. 'I did.'

'But you're not professional?'

'I could be, but I'm on other jobs, so dancing is my hobby. Think it's bad?'

'Of course not.' There were so many different kinds of dancing—luckily she knew them all. Spanish fandangos, Irish dances, Russian, Italian . . .

'Some you'll dance alone. I was told you were exceptionally good at that.'

11

Elaine wondered if Tommy had told him, but if so, why wasn't Garvin Humfrey mentioning Tommy? Should she? No, she decided. Tommy was a man, he must live his own life.

'I love dancing,' she agreed.

'So do I—but that doesn't make one a good dancer.'

She looked round the attractive room with the green murals of sea scenes and lovely trees and gardens on the walls and a bar at the far end. Through the windows, she could see the deck and the sea, cut up with small waves flecked with white foam. It was getting near time for the first dinner, so she should be going to have a bath and change.

Then she glanced at the list she had been given. 'The only trouble is,' she said worriedly, 'I didn't know I'd have to do this sort of dancing, so I haven't brought my Spanish or Russian clothes with me and only four evening gowns.'

'Not to worry. You'll find a case in your cabin of suitable clothes—Spanish, and the lot.'

'You . . . you got them? But how did you know my . . . size?'

He smiled. 'I asked and was told twelve. I thought at first it was your age, but then I twigged what it really was. If they don't fit, there's a dressmaker on board to alter it. We're at the same table, so I'll see you at dinner,' he finished, standing and opening the door, standing back to let her go out first.

She hurried along to the lift which was, as usual, full. It took her down, deep into the depths of the liner. The corridors all looked the same and she felt lost as she looked for her cabin—finally crossing to the other side of the ship and finding it. If Garvin Humfrey was on the Directors' Board, he probably had a suite on the top deck or near the Captain's. The stewards were busy, running baths, getting to know their passengers. As she went to open her cabin door, she saw Garvin Humfrey himself, come striding down the corridor, his face red with fury.

'You weren't supposed to bring a boy-friend,' Garvin Humfrey said, his voice thick with anger. 'I thought you would understand that.'

'My boy-friend?' She was startled. 'I have no . . .' Could it be Dirk? she thought, suddenly hopeful. Then Garvin Humfrey could leave them to do the dancing—which she would much prefer, for that would be fun.

'He was asking for you at the Purser's office. I hurried down to tell you to remember you are employed as a *dancer* and that this is not just a holiday for you. Your job comes first. Is that understood?' His voice rose as if his anger was more than he could control.

'Of course I know that. Who is it?' said Elaine, equally angry at the way Garvin

13

Humfrey spoke to her.

'An actor. Michael West.'

'Michael . . .? Oh no!'

'Oh yes. Then you know him?'

'Yes, I do know him, but . . . but I thought he was mad at me.'

'Mad at you? Why should he be?'

Elaine twisted her hands together. 'Well—he wants me to try for television or the theatre. He'd arranged for an audition, but I had to cancel it when I took this job.'

'You—an actress?' Garvin Humfrey's voice was sarcastic.

'No—a dancer. He says I'm exceptionally good.'

'Well, we'll see, won't we? What does he want? He can only have come on this ship for one reason—to be with you. What does he want if he isn't in love with you?'

'I haven't a clue,' said Elaine. 'He . . . I . . . well, we've been out several times and he's seen me dancing, but there was never more to it than that.'

'Well then, don't let there be. You're here to work, not to play,' Garvin Humfrey said curtly, and turned and walked away.

Elaine went into her small but adequate cabin thoughtfully. Why had Mike followed her? It didn't make sense, somehow. He had been angry, complained of being let down by her, said it was a fine way of showing gratitude after he had managed to arrange the audition

. . . then he had shrugged his shoulders and walked away as if it really didn't matter, after all! And now he was here.

The large suitcase on the floor was a new one, not hers, so it could only be the clothes Garvin Humfrey had said would be there. She knelt down and opened it—lifting out the dresses one after the other, each with a coat-hanger. Not that she had a great deal of room in the cabin, but . . .

She gasped with amazement as she looked at them. They were too beautiful for words must have cost a fortune. But then they weren't bought for *her* but to please the passengers on the liner.

There was a knock on her door, an arrogant, imperative knock. It could only be Mike, Elaine thought, as she went to open it.

But it wasn't. It was Garvin Humfrey again.

'I came to tell you, in case you didn't know,' he said, his voice sarcastic, 'that on the first night we don't dress up for dinner. It isn't *done.*'

CHAPTER TWO

After a quick bath, she returned to her cabin and put on her green trouser suit, as the yellow dress was simply for her practising hours. She brushed her hair and wondered whether or not to pile it high on her head as she did when dancing. She decided to let it hang down, tied back with a ribbon to match the suit, deciding that if she had an elaborate hair-do Garvin would probably make a sarcastic remark about 'dressing up'. Not that it mattered what he said, but at the same time, she didn't feel in the mood for his sarcasm.

She had hung up all the beautiful dresses and her hands kept touching them lovingly, admiring the softness of the silk and satin, the smartness of the design, the beauty of them. Some time she must try them all on, for it wouldn't do to find they didn't fit at the last moment! Then there would be a row. She'd go to bed early that night and try the dresses on first. Almost lovingly she stroked the Spanish silk. She loved Spanish dances and saw that in the suitcase were the castanets she would need. He seemed to have thought of everything.

Suddenly she heard the melodious notes of the gong. The first dinner! She didn't want to arrive late and walk in with everyone's eyes on her, so she hastily made up and hurried out of the cabin. Fortunately she was only one deck above the dining-room, so she went down the stairs and along the corridor until she came to the wide open glass doors and the carpeted steps down into the dining-room. Already most of the seats were taken and the Chief Steward came to meet her with a smile.

'I'm number twenty-three,' she said, and he pointed to a table a short way across the room. Her smile died quickly as she stared at the three people sitting there, leaving one chair— for her—vacant.

It couldn't be true, she thought at once. Yet it was. There sat Garvin Humfrey, studying the menu, and sitting by him was Mike with a glass in his hand as he talked to the girl by his side.

The girl!

Elaine turned away, tempted to hide, but Garvin had seen her and stood up and lifted his hand to beckon her. Somehow she made her reluctant legs move, but each step was an effort. She just could not understand how it could happen—in any case, how was it they were all at the same table?

The girl, strikingly beautiful with honey-gold hair and high cheekbones, was Felicity Holmes, Tommy's girl-friend, the one who had come with him to the monthly dances organised by Elaine's mother and who had often seen Elaine dance. But why was she here? Was she with Garvin Humfrey, Tommy's

17

guardian? Did she know where Tommy was? And if so, would she tell Garvin?

Tommy had vanished two weeks before. Just vanished as if he'd been whisked away by a fairy godmother. The police had looked for him—his photo had been in the paper, the hospitals searched, but there was no sign of Tommy. Elaine had not been worried; she had been delighted, for it meant to her that Tommy was growing up, that he wanted to lead his own life in his own way, not having to keep on asking his guardian for help. It had seemed to her that Tommy had become a man at last. But Felicity was his girl-friend, he had spent all his money on her, and she always wanted more. Now, for the first time, Elaine knew fear. Was Tommy in trouble—was he ill somewhere and unknown . . . ?

As she drew closer to the table, she thought bitterly how sorry she was for Tommy. There was something endearing in his youthfulness, his inability to make his own decisions. Not that *they* cared, she thought as she watched the way Felicity was laughing with Mike and the indifferent look on Garvin Humfrey's face. No one cared about Tommy.

Except herself. Not that she was in love with him. He was far too young a man for her to love in that way, but she still loved him, more as a concerned sister, or even, perhaps, a mother.

The thought made her smile as she reached

the table, for he was older than she was. Mike was on his feet at once, welcoming her. Garvin passed her the menu, introduced Felicity to her. Felicity smiled briefly and then turned again to Mike to talk to him. As Elaine studied the menu, she wondered why Felicity had pretended they had never met.

It was an uncomfortable meal. Felicity was flirting with both men and they seemed to enjoy it as she turned her lovely face first to the left and then to the right, teasing them, making them laugh, fluttering her eyelashes, while Elaine sat quietly, hardly speaking at all. Not that anyone seemed to notice that, for she was left alone, to sit miserably thinking that this would happen for fourteen days. Three meals a day, and that meant forty-two horrible meals! She also could see that neither Mike nor Garvin liked one another—there was a silent hostility there that made its subtle way out in their conversation or their voices.

It was a relief when they had finished eating and Garvin stood up and looked at her.

'Come on, Elaine, we have work to do.' He looked at the others. 'We'll see you anon.'

'But you're not dancing until half-past nine,' said Felicity, almost accusingly. 'Why must you go now?'

'Because we have a lot to discuss,' Garvin said patiently. 'Elaine and I only met a few hours ago and we have to work out the programme.'

'You don't need to worry about her,' Mike joined in, rubbing his hand through his dark hair. 'She's a super dancer.'

'It'll be interesting to see,' was Garvin's reply, and Elaine was filled with the desire to defy him—to tell him what he could do with his precious ship and that she was sick to death of his insulting, insinuating remarks . . . She felt the anger growing inside her, but before she could speak, his hand was under her arm and she was being almost lifted out of the dining-room, up the stairs, and then he let go of her. 'You've tried on the dresses?' he asked curtly.

'I haven't had time. I was going to do it later tonight.'

'What about the ones you have to wear tonight?'

Her hand went to her mouth guiltily, for he was right.

'We'll go now and you can try them on,' he said, leading the way up the staircase and to her cabin, opening the door and looking round. 'Not bad,' he said. 'You're surprisingly tidy.' He took the long piece of typed paper out of his pocket. 'Now let's see —we start with a tango.' He looked at the dresses thoughtfully, touching them gently, then lifted one down. 'How about this for the tango?'

Elaine loked at the deep red satin dress with its halter neck and a deceptively demure, straight skirt that was split up on either side

20

towards the waist.

'It is lovely,' she said.

'Well, try it on,' he told her, giving her the dress. He saw her startled face and burst out laughing. 'I'll wait outside—open the door when I can come in.' Still chuckling, he left the cabin, closing the door. Then opened and spoke round it, not looking in. 'Don't take too long. I've a lot to do this evening.' He closed the door again and her hands began to shake as she took off her trouser suit. There was no need to panic, she kept telling herself, she couldn't be faster than the fastest she could be, but her hands were still shaking as she hastily put on the dress. It fell in beautiful lines round her. It could have been made for her, it was such a perfect fit. In front of the mirror, she danced some steps and loved the flowing movement of the satin.

She opened the door and Garvin Humfrey came in. 'Not bad,' he said. 'Turn round . . . head up. You stoop rather a lot, you know.'

'Do I?'

'Yes. Rather like an ostrich—your head stretched out eagerly as if you're either starving or looking for someone you love.'

Her cheeks burned. 'I'll try to remember.'

'Your hair, too . . .'

She put her hands under the cloud of fair hair and lifted it.

'I always put my hair up when I dance.'

'Good. Tonight we'll do the conventional

dances: tango, one-step, and waltz. I suggest you have this one for the one-step,' he said, taking down another dress which was very modern with a halter neck and a long skirt of a patterned material, with reds, white, yellow and green; mixed as only an artist could do. 'What do you say?'

'It looks fine. I wish we'd had longer to practise the one-step.'

'Not to worry,' he told her. 'I was a bit rough with you this afternoon,' he added with a smile. 'Try to trust me. I'll be outside when you're ready,' he said as he opened the door.

'Hullo, Garvin,' a feminine voice said, but the door shut before Elaine could see who it was. It had sounded very much like Felicity.

Elaine took off the red satin dress and put on the modern one, opening the door.

He came in and nodded. 'That's good. Now for the waltz, we want something more romantic. What about this?'

He lifted down a dress that was absolutely unique. The bodice was cross-over in front, but there was none at the back, the frill round the neck holding the dress up. The skirt was made of layers of net of every shade of blue, from the palest to the deepest, almost purple, blue.

'It's beautiful!' she smiled.

He opened the cabin door. 'Try it on.'

She obeyed and when she called and he came in, she was staring in the mirror.

'Not bad,' he said curtly. 'Well, that's settled, then.'

She swung round. 'I'm not dancing alone?'

He shook his head. 'Not tonight.'

She flushed. 'You want to see if I can dance?'

He laughed. 'Exactly. I also am wondering if you get butterflies. Many do.'

'I do . . . sometimes. It depends.'

'On whom you're dancing with? Now if I were the great Dirk . . .'

'It's just that we've danced a lot together and . . .'

'We haven't at all. By the end of the voyage, you'll say differently. You're not a bad dancer,' he added kindly as if talking to an unhappy child. He looked at his watch. 'Sit down. I want to talk to you.'

She obeyed, being careful not to crumple the net layers.

'Did you know Michael West was going to sit at our table?' Garvin asked.

'Of course not.' She was startled by the sudden question. 'I was surprised when I saw him. I don't want him to.'

'Why not? Quarrelled?'

'Not really, though he was cross because I had to turn down the audition he had arranged for me, but I had no idea he was going to be on this ship, and I can't think why he is.'

'He seems rather taken with Felicity Holmes. Attractive, isn't she?'

23

'Very,' Elaine said, and it was the truth. Felicity had that charm, that ability to talk and listen to men, the right kind of smile and everything that appealed to a man.

'Well, maybe she'll keep Michael West out of your way, because we have a lot of work to do and I don't want him spoiling it.'

'I won't let him,' Elaine promised.

'Good.' He stood up. 'At nine o'clock I'll send a steward down for the clothes. Put them in the case. I've arranged for you to have somewhere you can change. Shoes okay? They're difficult to buy without being tried on.'

'Oh yes, thanks.'

'Good. Do what you like now, but watch the clock and be here not later than nine o'clock. The steward will show you the way.'

'I will,' she said, and closed the door on him.

Slowly she got out of the fragile-looking dress and put on her trouser suit. She looked at her watch. She had about half an hour and she felt like some fresh air. She would go up and take a walk round one of the decks.

It was quite quiet on the deck and the waves were much bigger—rolling towards the ship, the white froth tossing high. The air was fresh and invigorating, like a tonic. Just what she needed, she suddenly realised, for she had, after all, what Garvin had called 'butterflies'. It was quite an ordeal—dancing before curious, critical eyes with a man you hardly know and with whom you've only danced once. True, he had admitted being tough with her that afternoon and she knew he would be more helpful before an audience.

She stopped dead, moving back into the shadow of a lifeboat as she saw a couple come out on deck. It was Garvin himself—laughing and talking to . . . ? Felicity Holmes, of course. Who else! Certainly he didn't look as if he had butterflies.

Elaine managed to quietly slip through the heavy door and down to her cabin. There she brushed her hair vigorously, sweeping it up on to the top of her head, her hands knowing just what to do, having done it so often. Carefully she packed the dresses, her shoes and the make-up, and was ready when the steward came for her.

They went to what was quite a small room but sufficiently big enough for one person, so she quickly changed into the red satin gown. A mirror had been propped up on a table so she could do her face. She could hear voices and laughter from the central hall and the music the band was playing.

A knock came on the door and she opened it. Garvin stood there, looking incredibly handsome in his black tails. He smiled:

'Okay?'

Elaine nodded and went with him. One of the ship's officers met them with a smile. Then he announced to the packed hall the dancers and the drums rolled as Garvin took her hand

and led her forward. The lights were low except for one bright stream of light that centred on the dancers. The audience was just a blur of faces and she knew a moment of panic. If only it had been Dirk!

And then the music began—the beautiful yet arrogant music of the tango, and Garvin's arm went round her and his hand clasped her firmly. She knew a moment of fear as he started to dance—his long arrogant strides that took them over the floor so smoothly. In a few moments the magic of the music took possession of her and she was no longer nervous but could let herself enjoy the rhythm, the strength of his arms, the smile on his face. She had always loved the tango—but this was quite the nicest she had ever known.

It seemed as if the audience thought so too, for their applause was tremendous and went on and on as the two dancers bowed, retreated and returned to bow again, Garvin's hand tightly round Elaine's. Finally they got away and Garvin walked with her to the little room.

'That was good,' he said. 'Damn good. I really enjoyed it. Now change as fast as you can—the band plays a piece of music while we change—or rather, you do. We'll do the one-step next.'

She caught her breath as the pleasure that had filled her at his words of praise now vanished, for the one-step was a dance that needed hours of practice, especially with a new partner.

Perhaps Garvin knew this, because before he left her, he smiled and said: 'Don't worry— I'll play it gentle.'

Her hands were shaking a little as she hastily changed into the gay modern gown. She studied her face carefully. Did she look as nervous as she felt? She hoped not. The one-step needed such precision, such confidence, such speed and practice.

When Garvin knocked on the door, she opened it and he had a glass in his hand. 'Have a drink,' he said. 'It'll help.'

She wasn't sure that it would or that it might have a reverse effect and make her feet clumsy and her mind sleepy, but she swallowed it and the hot burning of her throat slowly vanished. Then he took her hand in his, and his words helped her far more than the drink had done.

'Don't worry,' he said. 'I have complete confidence in you.'

Again the Second Officer announced them and this time there was a surge of expectant applause and the drums rolled as Garvin took her forward, taking her in his arms as the happy gay music filled the hall. As he had promised, he played it so gently that she soon found her confidence and her feet were as nimble and understanding as his own. From a terrifying ordeal, it had become a joyous game and she was laughing happily as the audience applauded them with shouts as well as clapping. Again Elaine and Garvin had difficulty in getting away, but as they walked to her changing room, he said: 'That was fun, wasn't it?'

It was a far greater compliment than any praise could have been and she turned to him eagerly. 'I enjoyed every moment of it.'

The waltz, of course, was more sedate and more romantic—the dress so lovely with its layers of different shades of blue, and the audience clapped and clapped until their hands must have ached.

Staying in the lovely dress, Elaine went with Garvin to sit with the Captain's group. He was a charming man, surprisingly young, and full of praise for her dancing. Later she danced with him and with other passengers, all admiring her dress and her dancing.

All the time, though, she was waiting. Waiting for Mike to come and say why he was there on the ship. But then she didn't see Felicity Holmes either, so Elaine concluded that Felicity and Mike were not interested in the dancing but enjoying each other's company in one of the many bars. This was a relief, for Mike had a quick temper and might still be angry with her—also he had a horrible and irritating habit of arguing with a kind of pompous affectation. She decided to try to avoid seeing Mike—on such a large ship it shouldn't be difficult.

Back in her cabin, she set her alarm clock,

as she had to meet Garvin at seven a.m. She got into bed and fell asleep at once, for one of her biggest problems was solved—though she disliked Garvin, she loved dancing with him.

CHAPTER THREE

Elaine was awake before the alarm went off. She washed and dressed quickly, putting on the yellow dress. She hurried up to the top deck and Garvin was waiting for her outside the Green Bar, smoking as he looked over the rail on the deck. He smiled.

'Punctual, for once?'

'I'm always punctual!'

'Let's hope so. Sleep well?'

'Fine, thanks.'

They went into the big beautifully decorated room, all the chairs piled down the side. 'We've only got an hour and then they'll be cleaning it,' Garvin said as he sorted out some records. 'I thought we'd do the Apache dance.' He looked up with a smile. 'You know it, of course.'

'Of course. It's great.'

'I want us to do a slow foxtrot first so that its dignity will contrast with the virility and violence of the Apache dance.'

'It sounds good.'

It was a pleasant hour—Elaine loved every

minute of it. She had often danced these dances with Dirk, but it was even more alive, more expressive of the music than she had ever known. By the time they finished, her cheeks were red with heat, her hair a mess falling over her face, but her eyes were shining. Garvin looked at his watch. 'Help, we're going to be late! I'm starving. What about you?'

Elaine was stretching her arms, her graceful movements showing the beauty of her body.

'Yes, I am hungry,' she said, 'but that was such fun.'

'You certainly enjoy dancing,' he commented as they went to the lift.

She smiled, 'So do you.'

'Mine is just a hobby—a means of relaxing in this world of difficulties and unsolvable problems.'

'Dancing is my life,' she said simply.

He looked at her. 'You're not serious? Don't you want to marry and have children?'

She laughed. 'Of course I do, one day, but I want to dance round the world before I have them.'

'So your career comes first?'

The way he said it startled her—it was almost as if he was not only shocked but disgusted.

She thought of Tommy and clenched her hands. She must not mention his name or let Garvin know she knew his ward. 'Is there anything wrong in being ambitious?' she asked.

Poor Tommy, drifting through life, not knowing what he wanted to do.

'Of course not—but a woman's place is at home,' Garvin said quickly.

Elaine laughed. 'You're out of date. I agree in a way, but let us live first.'

'You don't think mother-and-wifehood is living?' he asked, his voice suddenly cold.

She looked at his blond hair and blue eyes that seemed to clash with the brown of his sun-kissed skin.

'Of course it is,' she said, beginning to feel annoyed. 'When the right time comes.'

'What age would you advise?' he asked sarcastically.

'I'd say thirty or thirty-two, but it all depends.'

'Depends on what?'

'Whether or not I'd met someone I wanted to marry.'

'I see—you're selective?' He sounded amused. which annoyed her still more.

'And why not? Marriage is the most difficult partnership in life. You've got to be sure.'

'You're so right,' he agreed, and startled her by the change in his voice; the sarcasm and amusement had vanished. 'That's why I've never ventured into its seductive but dangerous arms.'

'You've never been in love?'

He smiled. 'Of course, a hundred times, but never enough to make it worth the risk.'

They had reached the dining-room by now and she saw that their table was empty. Obviously Felicity slept late and it looked as if Mike preferred a Continental breakfast in his cabin. She was glad neither of them were there—glad also that Garvin had lost his sarcasm.

They sat down and both ordered coffee, orange juice and scrambled eggs with bacon and mushrooms. Toast was immediately put on the table in case they were desperately hungry. It seemed that Garvin was, as he helped himself after offering the toast rack to Elaine. When the steward had gone, Garvin asked a question quietly—one that was hard to answer.

'What do you look for in a husband?'

She was so startled she nearly dropped her piece of toast.

'I don't know. I hadn't thought of it.'

'You must have—a girl like you who's continually mixing with men must have amorous boy-friends at times. Don't tell me no one has asked you to marry him?'

Her cheeks burned. 'In a way, but not exactly a proposal.'

'Dirk Long?' he asked, and when she shook her head, he asked: 'Mike?'

Elaine looked a little worried. 'Please don't say anything, because he didn't actually ask me to marry him.'

'I suppose he's anti-marriage. Are you?'

She shook her head violently, the cloud of fair hair swinging.

'Most certainly not,' she said, then blushed, for she had been told by so many that she was square and out of date. 'I'm thinking of the children,' she added.

'The children . . .' Garvin said thoughtfully. 'Do you think that in this day and age it matters?'

'I honestly don't know, but how can I tell my daughter about the dangers of drugs and easy love when she knows I've lived for years with her father and not bothered to get married?'

'So you believe parents should set good examples to their children?'

'Well, what's wrong with that?' she asked angrily. 'It's from our parents that we learn what's right and wrong.'

'My, what a responsibility you give to parents!'

His amused voice irritated her. 'And why not? You shouldn't be a parent unless you're prepared to take the responsibilities.'

He pulled a wry face. 'My, you're going to be a strict mother!'

'I am not. Just loving and understanding and teaching them to be independent, able to stand on their own feet,' Elaine began indignantly, and suddenly realised what she was saying, so stopped abruptly. 'Like my mother,' she finished.

Garvin looked at her as the plates were slid

in front of them.

'At last! Your father?'

'He died a few years ago. They've been wonderful parents. That's really why I took this job and gave up the chance of the audition—Mother is working hard to build up her school of dancing, and this . . .' Elaine waved her hand expressively: 'This is good publicity.'

'You still haven't told me what you expect of your husband,' Garvin said unexpectedly as he began to eat as if starving.

Elaine looked at him and gave an innocent smile. 'What I expect or what I'd like?'

'Touché!' said Garvin, and roared with laughter so loudly that people at tables around them turned to stare. 'I asked for that,' he went on.

He was smiling for the rest of breakfast, talking about the dances, and Elaine really enjoyed the meal. She only wished that Felicity and Mike need never join them. When Garvin was talking about dancing, he was a different person, so relaxed and friendly, and Elaine wished he could always be like that.

As they finished breakfast, he changed again, becoming curt as he said: 'Look, do what you like this morning—it's too cold yet to swim—but steer clear of Michael West. I don't like that bloke. I'll see you at lunch and then at two we'll have another hour of practice. I thought you might like to do the Spanish

34

dance tonight. Would you care to rehearse or do you know it well enough?'

'Actually, I'd like to rehearse with the orchestra. There's the timing and . . .'

'I know. I'll arrange for them to come.' He stood up and she followed him.

They separated in the lift and Elaine hurried to her cabin, eager to brush and discipline her hair and to change out of the yellow dress into her green trousers and a warm white sweater.

First she went to the writing-room and wrote to her mother, telling her she couldn't understand Dirk's behaviour. 'Surely he could have written and told us. I had such a shock, or is he ill?' Elaine wrote, then added that the partner she had was an even better dancer than Dirk.

'He's wonderful when he's dancing or talking about it. I shall be glad to be home,' she wrote, then wondered if that was true. She enjoyed every moment she spent in Garvin's arms or discussing dancing with him. If only they could dance all the time!

There were quite a lot of couples pacing up and down the deck where it was cold, surprisingly so when you looked up at the cloudless blue sky. She did hope it wasn't going to rain or snow or spoil their holidays which probably meant so much to these old people. She had a book to read and was looking for a sheltered corner when turning at the stern of the ship she bumped into of all people!—Mike.

'Hullo,' he said, and he didn't sound too pleased to see her, but then neither was she, knowing his quick tempers and the cruel things he could say. 'How did you get on last night? I can't bear to see a man like Humfrey dancing. Makes me sick.'

'He's fond of dancing—'

'Or the girls he dances with,' Mike said scornfully. 'Watch out, Elaine. You're an innocent child and he's an experienced womaniser.'

'He's nothing like that with me,' she said quickly.

'That's his line. Go slowly, but he'll get there in the end. You didn't tell me he was to be your partner. Why not? Is that why you took the job? He's well known for his wealth.'

'I didn't know. I thought Dirk, my usual partner, would be here.'

'Why isn't he?'

'Haven't a clue. Maybe he's ill. He was on holiday, perhaps he's stayed on in Morocco.'

'How do you get on with Humfrey?' Mike asked.

'Fine. He loves dancing as much as I do.'

'Dancing! That's a new name for it.' He looked out at the sea with the long waves coming towards them with a dignified speed and strength. 'Still cold. What are you going to do?'

'Read—and rest. We had an hour's practice and have another hour after lunch. Then we teach after tea and dance late tonight.'

'You're certainly earning your money. It must be unutterably boring.'

'Of course it isn't, Mike. Would you say acting was boring? You know you wouldn't. Yet I find your shop talk very dull.'

'You never said so.'

'Of course not—besides, it's not when you're talking to me but when you're with other actors and I don't know what it's all about. Same with us. We speak the same language.'

He grunted. He was a short man, slightly plump, but with a handsome face, dark hair, sideboards, and dark eyes. He was only in his late twenties, but somehow he looked older. 'Well, watch out, that's all I say, Elaine. You're too young to cope with men like that.'

'Mike! I was surprised to see you.'

He smiled. 'I bet you were!'

'Why did you come?'

He laughed. 'That's a question I can't answer, but I promise you one thing, it wasn't to chase you. See you later.' He lifted his hand and walked off.

Elaine found her way to the stern of the ship and a sheltered corner and was lucky enough to find a chair. She sat down, the sun that had so little warmth yet shining on her as she opened her book. At least, she thought, that was one blessing. Mike was not interested in her.

But that left a question in her mind. *Why* was he here? He had always spoken scornfully of these short cruises. Just a waste of time and money, he had said. So why was he here?

CHAPTER FOUR

The next few days were a mixture of joy and misery to Elaine. The sun appeared and the swimming-pool was crowded and so was the deck nearby as the passengers lay in the sun, determined to enjoy every moment of it. Elaine swam quite a lot; she also went to the gymnasium, played games on the decks, had someone to talk to, for the dancing lessons in the afternoon had introduced her to many interesting people. The misery part was meal times. Breakfast was perfect, for then she and Garvin were alone and could talk—but the other meals were misery for Elaine as she sat silently, never speaking, though no one seemed to notice, for Felicity just ruled the roost, doing all the talking to each man, deliberately baiting one and with skill making him blame the other man for it. She was also clever at starting a conversation on something she knew they felt strongly about and it would end in what was uncomfortably nearly a row, to Elaine's dismay.

She had told Garvin what Mike had said. 'But why is he on the ship?' Garvin asked at once.

'I don't know. I did ask him that and he said he couldn't tell me, but he was not chasing me.'

'I see. You're sorry?'

She laughed. 'No, I'm relieved. Mike and I . . . no, I'm not sorry. It means I'm free to enjoy my leisure hours.'

Garvin looked thoughtful. 'I wonder if . . . Yes, I think I can guess what Mike's after. That means I have a rival.'

She had begun to repeat how Mike had said he wasn't chasing her, but she had stopped in time, realising that she had nearly implied that Garvin was chasing her—which was the least likely of anything. If she had gone on . . . oh, what an opportunity for his sarcasm it would have been! But she had wondered what Garvin would say if she told him that Felicity—who seemed to attract him very much—was the girl-friend of Tommy, the girl who had made him spend his money, and often Garvin's too! It was also strange that Felicity was on this type of voyage —normally she went yachting in the Mediterranean with her wealthy friends.

The dancing lessons were fun—after tea when many passengers came to line up while Garvin and Elaine demonstrated the different dances and taught them how to dance them.

Garvin and Elaine would also dance with the pupils and a lot of laughter and chatting made it a friendly, pleasant task.

Of course Elaine's happiest moment was the evening dancing—in Garvin's arms, having him smile at her, knowing that he was enjoying it as much as she was.

There was a cinema show every afternoon as well as evening, but most passengers preferred to lie in the sunshine and enjoy it while they could. After the dancing, there would be bridge for those who liked it, or bingo, which was much more popular. Elaine usually vanished at this time, as she hated bingo, and if she didn't meet any passenger who asked her to dance with him at one of the bars, she would go down to her cabin.

The incident after her Spanish dance had made her do that. The dance had been exhilarating as her gold-frilled white dress swung as she danced, her hands held high as she clicked the castanets and her body swayed as she was caught in the magic of the music. The applause was terrific and after a quiet modern dance with Garvin, he told her the Spanish dance was so appreciated, he suggested they danced one together. They had not rehearsed it, but he said he felt sure they both knew what to do . . .'Wear the other dress,' he said, and she had agreed, eager to dance such an alive, warm dance. She wore a white and red dress, the frills on the skirt being

40

dotted with black spots. He wore a black suit and a bright red cummerbund and as the drums rolled and they walked on, his fingers warm round hers, she was so happy . . .

It was a lively dance—the castanets clicking, Elaine's frills whirling against Garvin's dark suit. When he held her in his arms, she felt the warmth of them and his smile seemed to mean more than he had ever said as they both relaxed and gave themselves to the music. In the end the audience were clapping to the beat of the music, many shouting 'Olé . . . olé!' excitedly.

Afterwards she had danced in one of the bars with a tall man with dark hair. He was also a good dancer and she was quite tired when he suggested they went out on deck.

'It is hot, is it not?' he asked with his slight accent.

'Yes, it is,' she agreed.

The decks were empty, as most of the passengers were playing bingo or bridge, or in the cinema. She didn't know the man's name and it was difficult to talk to him, for he obviously spoke English more easily than he understood it. The moon was high in the sky, sending a silver pathway across the huge powerful waves that came whirling and fast towards the ship. They leaned over the rail, an awkward silence growing longer when suddenly his arms went round her and he was bending her backwards with the fierceness of his kiss. Never had she been kissed with such violence, such demand, and though she struggled, his arms tightened round her.

'Sorry to interrupt, Elaine, but we're wanted in the Captain's cabin,' said Garvin, suddenly appearing by their side.

The unknown man's arms fell to his side. 'Some other time?' he said with a smile and a little bow, and hurried down the deck.

Breathless, Elaine leant against the rail, rubbing her hand gently over her bruised mouth.

'For crying out loud,' Garvin snapped. 'Isn't it time you grew up? Surely you know how to cope with those Don Juan's? You women make me mad! You dress and make up and dance to entice us, and when we fall for your charms, you're furious and fight us. I'm sorry for the poor devil. He fell for you all right!'

'But you don't kiss someone you don't even know,' Elaine protested.

'Don't you?' Garvin smiled. 'Maybe you don't, but we do.'

'But . . . but there's no love in it.'

'Has there to be love in every kiss?' he asked.

She glared at him. 'I think so.'

'Well, I don't,' Garvin said, and suddenly she was in his arms, his mouth moving over hers as he demanded a response. What shocked her was that she found herself returning his kisses, her body relaxed. It was

42

some time before he let her go, gently. 'Sorry about that,' he said with a smile, 'but I'm only a man. Now I must go. Just watch out. I won't always be around.'

'The Captain's cabin?'

He laughed. 'Just a tactful excuse to break up the scene.'

Elaine managed a laugh. 'Very clever of you! I've got a bit of a headache, so I think I'll go down below to my cabin.'

'Good idea.' As they walked towards the heavy-to-open door from the deck, he looked down at her. 'I enjoyed that dance.'

She smiled at him. 'So did I. Very much.'

'So did the audience. Look, Elaine, you're very young for your age—do watch out and find an excuse for not going on moonlit decks. Just remember that men are men—and we think you're inviting romance.'

'Just walking on a dark deck?' She had sounded sceptical.

'You agreed to come outside—that was as good as an invitation. Good-bye for now,' he added, and left her.

She had gone down to her cabin, refusing a few offers of a drink and a dance on her way. She was remembering what Garvin had said:

'Has there to be love in every kiss?'

He had kissed her and she knew he didn't love her; if he loved anyone, it was Felicity.

And—she realised suddenly—she, too, had kissed him. Would he remember what she had said, and would he see that kiss she had given him as a sign that she loved him?

Was it?

She had tossed and turned in bed that night, remembering every event of the evening, going over the lovely moments as they danced—the wonderful moments as he kissed her—and then the words he had said. Not cruel—just truthful. But what about herself? Why had she kissed him?

It was because of that mixed-emotion evening that kept her away from decks at night and sent her to her cabin early, for Garvin and Mike were always hovering round Felicity while she flirted cleverly with them both. It was very obvious to the passengers and several had said sympathetically to Elaine that it was just 'too bad' and she had explained that there was no romance between her and Garvin. Some of them looked amused, others told her she was a brave little girl, but how many believed her? she wondered.

It was a beautiful ship and life on it was ideal—at least Elaine thought so. Garvin said it reminded him of boarding school, for you were told what to do, what time to eat, and entertainment was arranged for you. What was wrong with that? Elaine asked him, and he laughed.

'I'm a loner and like to eat when I feel like it, not when I'm told to.'

'But it's so relaxing.'

'I'm glad you find it so.'

Elaine did—she loved standing by the rail watching the patterns formed by the waves as they came racing to the ship—she loved the birds that swooped down into the sea—the glimpse they had of several seals. She liked the colours of the walls and curtains, the comfortable seats, the good food. It was such fun to eat when you haven't paid for it . . . for in the past sometimes her own grocery bill had startled her. It was even worse with meat and fish and here she could have lobster and prawns and soles and steaks, beautifully tender, and gorgeous sweets, ices and soufflés. She was lucky in that she hadn't to worry about how much she ate, for she stayed slender and perfectly formed, as Garvin remarked casually one day.

'You're a natural dancer,' he said, 'with the perfect form.'

His compliments were rare, so she appreciated them more, and she wasn't surprised at how popular he was with the passengers. He was polite, even courteous in what might be called an old-fashioned way, but it was a way that delighted women, especially those no longer young.

One day they were talking and Fiona, the hard-working hostess, came hurrying to them.

'I don't know if you have time to spare, Garvin,' she said with her friendly smile. 'I haven't many problems, but there is one. An elderly couple who don't make friends easily, they seem to have nothing to say but "Yes", "No" or "Really?"—none of them exactly helpful. They just sit in silence, pretending to read. I can't help feeling they're lonely, and I can't have that.'

'What do you want me to do?' Garvin asked.

'I want you both to do it—' Fiona said with a smile at Elaine. 'Let me introduce you to them. They've both said how much they love your dancing and both were keen dancers before he fell ill and wasn't allowed to dance. Will you?' she asked, in that slightly pathetic, very pleading voice of hers that was one of the reasons of her success with the passengers.

'Of course,' said Garvin. 'Where are they?'

'In the smoking-room. It's quiet there. Come with me.' Fiona led the way and as they entered the big cool room with its leather armchairs and couches, Elaine saw a curious look on Garvin's face, noticed a slight hesitation in his walk, but then he seemed to overcome it as they followed Fiona.

The couple were elderly—in their seventies, Elaine guessed. The woman in a dark dress with a white lace collar and her white hair twisted round her head. She had a sad mouth, drooping at the corners. Her husband was a thin, pale man, completely bald, and with deep lines of suffering in his face. He put down his book as the three of them came

46

closer.

'Why, Miss Kent, what a nice surprise,' he said in a weary voice.

His wife put down the knitting she was doing and looked up.

'Oh no! How nice of you. You must be so busy,' she said, looking at Elaine.

'They'd like to meet you,' Fiona said with a smile.

'We're glad to meet you,' said the elderly woman, smiling too. 'You're the most beautiful dancers we ever saw. Aren't they, William?' she said, giving her silent husband a gentle nudge.

'Yes. Yes, of course they are. Quite the best,' he said obediently.

'Well, I'll introduce you. This is Elaine Thomas and this is Garvin Humfrey—I'd like you to meet Mr. and Mrs. Morris.'

Mrs. Morris sat upright. 'You're not one of the Cornish Humfreys?'

Garvin sat down and pointed to a chair near Mr. Morris for Elaine.

'Yes, I am. We lived at Carbis Bay.'

'Well!' Mrs. Morris said softly. 'You were a very young man last time I saw you. Your father had died and your mother was sick and you had to work to send your two young sisters to school and to feed you all. We said how tough it was for a young man, didn't we, William?' This time she didn't have to give her husband a gentle nudge, for he was looking

47

interested.

'We certainly did. You had a tough time, young man.'

Garvin smiled. 'Most of us have tough times, but we survive.'

'Too right. We have no choice,' William Morris agreed.

His wife was frowning a little. 'When we left Cornwall I didn't hear any more of you until your sister died. It was all in the papers.'

By chance, Elaine glanced at Garvin and saw the surprise and what looked like quickly controlled dismay on his face. 'It was very sad,' he said.

Mrs. Morris leaned forward. 'I'm sure it was, Garvin, I can remember when your sister married and everyone said he was too old for her.'

'Yes, his wife had been killed in a car crash. It was ironic, because that was how he died. He wasn't driving at the time, he had a chauffeur. He was very wealthy.'

'I remember that,' Mr. Morris said suddenly.

'A lot of people said she married him for his money, but that was a lie,' said Mrs. Morris.

'Absolutely. They were the happiest couple,' Garvin said quickly.

'He left all his money to her, didn't he?' William Morris suddenly said.

'Yes, he had no idea she would die so soon.'

'I read about it in the papers, Garvin, and I

was so sorry for you. A terrible thing for a young man of twenty-four.'

Elaine was a little puzzled. Had Garvin been so fond of his sister?

Mrs. Morris looked at Elaine with a smile. 'Tough on such a young man to find himself guardian of six children, isn't it.'

'Six?' Elaine echoed, really surprised. Tommy had never mentioned any sisters or brothers, and she had taken it for granted he was Garvin Humfrey's only ward. But six! 'That does sound hard.' She looked at Garvin and caught him staring at her with an odd expression, but immediately he turned to Mrs. Morris with a smile.

'Their grandmother looks after them. I'm just responsible for their financial welfare.'

'Did your sister leave it all to you?' Mr. Morris asked.

'I'm afraid so,' Garvin said with a sigh.

'Why are you afraid?' Mrs. Morris asked quickly.

'It was tough on their eldest son. I don't think he's ever forgiven me for inheriting the lot.'

Elaine nearly spoke, but clenched her hands as she stopped herself. Maybe Tommy was not the eldest child. If he was, then Garvin was quite wrong, for Tommy had never resented the will, he had even joked and said it was as well that his money had been put into a trust allowance by his guardian, as otherwise he

49

would have spent the lot within a year or so. But Garvin—poor Garvin at the age of twenty-four being landed with six children!

'That's unfair,' Mrs. Morris said. 'You didn't want to be guardian to six children.'

'Six?' Elaine echoed before she could stop herself. She stared at Garvin. 'Six?' she repeated.

He smiled, but there was a strange cold look in his eyes that puzzled her.

'Yes, six. Three boys and three girls.'

'My word!' she said softly. Why hadn't Tommy ever mentioned them?

'And they all fight like mad. How their grandmother copes with them, I don't know. They also happen to be very lovable,' Garvin said slowly. 'They also cause me a lot of worry. Take Tommy, for instance . . .'

Elaine's nails dug into the palms of her hands as she made herself sit still and say nothing, doing her best to look as if she had never heard of Tommy in her life.

'Yes, he's vanished, hasn't he?' said Mrs Morris. 'We read it in the papers, didn't we, William?' This time she had to give him quite a hard nudge, for he had dozed off.

'What? Yes, yes, of course . . .' he mumbled.

Mrs. Morris smiled ruefully. 'I'm afraid he always sleeps at this time. He has to take pills, and you know what they can do! Have you traced Tommy yet?' she asked anxiously.

'Not yet,' Garvin said, and his voice

hardened. 'But I'm hoping to soon. I have a very good idea who can tell me just where he is, and I mean to find him soon,' he said, a threat in his voice.

Did he know about Felicity, then? Elaine wondered. Was that why he spent so long with Felicity . . . would she tell him? And if so, would it help Tommy?

'What made him disappear like that?' Mrs. Morris asked.

'He was angry with me,' Garvin said, and Elaine looked at him in surprise she was too slow to control. Tommy had said nothing about that. 'He planned to get married and wanted more money. I said he was too young to marry and it was time he learned to live on his own money, not mine. He knew I meant what I said—so, like a child, he puts his finger to his nose and walks out, knowing I'll be worried sick.'

'He's a man, Garvin,' Mrs. Morris said gently.

'When is a man a man? I don't think it has anything to do with years.'

'I think it has more to do with behaviour and the way you're treated,' Elaine spoke for the first time, unable to keep quiet.

'Well, I'm sure he's been very well treated,' Mrs. Morris said quickly. 'What does he do?'

'He paints,' Garvin said, and Elaine had only just managed to stop herself from saying it.

51

'Is he good?'

'Not very,' said Garvin. 'But I think he will be—one day. When he's learned to live.'

He never will, Elaine wanted to say, until you treat him as a man. He has no self-confidence. You see him as a useless child and that's how he sees himself. Can't you see, Garvin? she wanted badly to say, but she must keep quiet about it.

After another half an hour, talking about life in Carbis Bay and Garvin's youth, Garvin asked to be excused and left Elaine with the sleeping husband and the talkative Mrs. Morris. How, Elaine wondered, could Fiona have thought Mrs. Morris couldn't talk? She barely stopped, with questions about Elaine's background, her work, her mother, the dancing school, her love of dancing.

'That was the hardest sacrifice I had to make,' Mrs. Morris said, 'when William became ill and wasn't allowed to dance. Garvin is a fine man, isn't he? Now, it must be tea time.'

Elaine stood up. 'Yes, I must go, because after tea we give dancing lessons. Why don't you join us? There are plenty of men.'

'Shall I?' Mrs. Morris's face lit up. 'I'd love to. William wouldn't mind, I'm sure.'

'Good. I'll see you at five o'clock,' Elaine said, saying good-bye and hurrying down to the dining-room for a much-needed cup of tea. Her mind was going over and over it again: why hadn't Tommy ever mentioned his five brothers and sisters? And Garvin—poor Garvin, only a year older than Tommy was now and landed with six wards. What a responsibility—no wonder he enjoyed the relaxation of dancing!

As she left the dining-room, she remembered what he had said:

'I have a very good idea who can tell me just where he is . . .' Was he talking of Felicity? Who else?

CHAPTER FIVE

That afternoon at the dancing lessons Elaine saw to it that Mrs. Morris had a nice partner. The men lined up opposite the 'girls' while Elaine and Garvin showed them the different dances and it was their job to make sure that each person had a partner. The joy on Mrs. Morris's face was more than repayment and her happiness when Garvin, himself, danced with her was quite something. Elaine tried to imagine how she would feel if she had to give up her beloved dancing because her husband wasn't allowed to dance . . . It would depend, of course, on how much you loved your husband.

'You knew Mrs. Morris well?' Elaine asked when the dancing class came to an end and they went to one of the bars for a cool drink.

He looked a little annoyed, to Elaine's surprise. 'Frankly, I don't remember her so well, but I remember him. She certainly seems to have taken an interest in our family,' he added sarcastically, then changed the subject so quickly that she realised that for some reason he didn't want to talk about the Morrises.

Much later that evening, after the dancing which had caused much applause and laughter, for they had done a spider and fly dance in which Elaine was the spider, seducing the fly who finally got away to the joy of the spectators, Elaine was dancing with an elderly but charming man who told her they would see land next day.

'I understand we stop at the island and get fresh fish aboard as well as fruit and vegetables. It'd be nice to step on solid ground for a few hours, but I'm afraid we can't. It should be pretty beautiful—palm trees and tropical flowers.'

'Why can't we go ashore?'

'I don't know. Maybe they don't want too many tourists to swarm over the island and spoil the paradise. It's not very big, so I heard, and is popular for honeymoons.' He chuckled. 'Just suit us, because we've been married forty years, so we reckon this is a sort of second honeymoon.'

Elaine smiled as the music stopped. 'I hope you'll both enjoy it very much.'

He laughed. 'We are—thanks.'

She looked across the room and saw Garvin was dancing with Felicity—as usual, Elaine thought bitterly, when he isn't dancing with one of the passengers. He always made for those who looked forlorn and lonely and she was supposed to do the same, but she was going to bed early, feeling forlorn herself, though she didn't know why. Mike was standing, arms folded, scowling as he watched them. Felicity was playing them off and obviously enjoying it.

Ever since the Morrises had spoken to them about him, Garvin had seemed annoyed as if he didn't like his private life examined. But why should he mind? She still could not get over the thought of a man' of twenty-four finding himself guardian to six children. Six! Was Tommy the eldest? she wondered, and again wondered why he had never mentioned his brothers or sisters.

As she undressed and got into bed, she thought that maybe it would do them all good to have a day ashore. However, perhaps there was no dock big enough for the liner or it was a small coral-surrounded lagoon and the waves too rough to have boats come and fetch the passengers. It was a pity, though . . . it might have shaken Garvin out of his sudden strange mood.

Next day the alarm woke her and she hastily dressed and hurried up to the deck where

Garvin was waiting impatiently.

'At last,' he said, almost crossly, which was unfair, for she was dead on time. Was he in one of his moods? It would spoil their dancing.

She went to the door, but Garvin's hand was on her arm.

'We're not dancing this morning,' he said. 'I've got a surprise for you. We're going ashore for a while.'

'We are?' she said, delighted, and looked out of the window. The ship was moving slowly, she realised, and she could see the island. It looked very lovely, with sandy coves and palm trees waving in the breeze. But it also looked as if there was no one living on the island, for there were no houses to be seen at all. There was a small hill covered with trees that made something like a screen so that little could be seen. 'I'm glad.'

Garvin gave her an odd look. 'You are? You knew about it?'

'I danced with Mr. Slater last night and he told me he wished the passengers could go ashore, as it was a lovely island. He'll be pleased the passengers are going, because he thought they wouldn't be allowed.'

'They aren't,' Garvin said.

'They're not? Oh, I am sorry. He and his wife have been married forty years and this is their second honeymoon. He said it was popular for honeymoons.'

Garvin's face relaxed as he laughed. 'I'd

hardly think so. No, the hoi-polloi can't go, but we're different. That's why we're going early, so that there are not many passengers about who might try to join us, which would spoil everything.'

'In what way?'

'Well, even if we tried, we couldn't get them all ashore. And those who couldn't go would resent it. Better for no one to go. Come on.'

He took her arm in his hand and hustled her down the stairs to one of the lower decks where several sailors stood and one of the officers came up to Garvin just as he was showing Elaine the two small schooners that were coming alongside the ship as it slowed down. 'We stop here to . . .' he began, then turned away to answer the question the Second Officer asked him quietly.

When they stopped speaking, Elaine put her hand on Garvin's arm.

'Have I time to go and change? This is my working dress.'

He looked her up and down. 'You look all right to me, so not to worry. No one dresses up here. Come along.'

It only took a few moments to get them on the deck of the schooner which immediately drew away from the liner and went towards the small lagoon which had an equally small jetty.

The nearer the island they got, the more beautiful it looked. Now she could see the purple and red and yellow flowers on the creepers that grew over the rocks that lined the sandy beaches. It was good of Garvin, she thought gratefully, turning to smile at him. He didn't smile back. His face had a strange look, his mouth was a thin line as if he was trying to control himself. Why, she knew not, but she was so happy that she wanted to tell him and thank him with all her heart for having been so thoughtful and letting her enjoy the beauty of this island, even though the passengers were denied it. Their dancing, she knew, had brought them closer together than a year's friendship could have done.

The schooner stopped at the jetty and soon Elaine and Garvin were walking ashore, past the only building in sight, which was a rather rickety-looking wooden hut that seemed to be dangerously balanced on the side of the hill. Apart from the schooner's crew, there wasn't a man or woman in sight, but there was an earth road that led away from the jetty and seemed to vanish in a mass of palm trees.

'This way,' said Garvin, pointing to a pathway that wended its way under the trees.

Elaine followed him, thinking that perhaps it was a short cut to a hotel, for there must be one if this was a favourite place for honeymooners.

When she saw the house, she had quite a shock. In the first place, it could hardly be called a house, since it was little more than a large hut built of wooden slabs. The roof was galvanised iron, but there was a wide verandah. There was a wild sort of garden round the hut, bright with flowers but also with weeds. She could hardly imagine a honeymoon couple staying there happily, but if . . .

'We'll stay on the verandah,' Garvin said. 'Sit down. I'll get us a cold drink.'

Elaine sat down on quite a comfortable chair. There was not much of a view, for they were surrounded by palm trees and creepers. He went inside the hut and she thought how strangely, almost eerily, quiet it was, then suddenly, as if a light had been switched on, the cicadas began to hum and some birds to sing. All the same there was a strange loneliness in the air—as if they were completely isolated from the world.

Garvin returned with two glasses of ice-cold lemonade. As he sat down, he looked at her and asked: 'Where's Tommy?'

She was so startled that she spoke before she could stop herself. 'I don't know.'

Garvin sat back and gave an odd smile. 'So you admit that you do know him?'

'And what if I do?' she asked, suddenly cross with him for the way he had tossed the question at her.

'Why didn't you tell me?'

'You didn't tell me you were worried about him.'

'You heard me tell Mrs. Morris I was.'

'Look, it was none of my business . . .'

59

'That's an odd way of putting it, seeing you're one of Tommy's closest friends,' he said, his voice cold as ice.

'I am not!'

'Is that so? Then why did he always go to your mother's monthly dances and never fail to watch you dancing?'

'How do you know?'

He shrugged his shoulders. 'How do you think? When Tommy suddenly vanished, I was worried sick, so I put a private detective on to make enquiries and your name came up. That's why you're here with me now.'

Elaine was so startled she leaned forward. 'I don't understand. What do you mean? Why I am here now?'

'I knew you would be on Tommy's side, and I wanted you to see mine. That's why I paid off Dirk not to come with you—indeed, that was why I hired you in the first place. Tommy's best friend and the only person that could help us to find him.'

'Us?'

He nodded. 'His grandmother nearly had a nervous breakdown, she was so worried about the boy.'

'That's the whole trouble,' Elaine said angrily. 'Tommy isn't a boy—he's a man. If only you would treat him as one and give him responsibilities instead of . . .'

'Instead of what?'

'Instead of making him dependent on you—

utterly. Not only for money but for solving his problems. He always goes to you for advice, doesn't he? No doubt you enjoy it—you're the type who'd like to be a patriarch, ruling the world. No one should be made so dependent!' Her voice rose a little as the anger flooded her. 'My parents taught me to stand on my feet from an early age and I'm very grateful to them. I've never been dependent in any way, yet I know if there was big trouble, I could go to them . . . to her. But Tommy . . . he can't make a decision without asking you first. I had a friend, Cleo, she was submissive and utterly dependent on her eldest sister, Margaret. When Margaret got married and went to live in South America, poor Cleo was lost. She couldn't even sign a cheque or buy a railway ticket, because Margaret had done everything. Now can you say that's right? I can't. If you weren't so generous with money, Tommy would *have* to get a job and earn a living. He needs that kind of responsibility. He's twenty-three and not thirteen,' she said bitterly. 'Why not treat him as a man? What'll happen when he marries? Will you keep them?'

'So you are going to marry him,' Garvin said slowly. 'That's what I thought, but . . .'

'I'm not marrying him. He's not my type.'

'What is your type?' he asked, and when she didn't answer, he went on: 'Well, he's got his trust allowance. If he marries before he can keep his own wife, he'll not get an extra penny from me. Where is he . . . ?' Garvin demanded, his face flushed with anger. 'Can't you see, we're worried to death about him. He's immature, weak, unable to say no, and we're afraid he may get caught up with a bad crowd and get on drugs. He's quite capable of that.'

Elaine hesitated. 'I don't think you're right there,' she said, her voice calm. 'I'm hoping he's suddenly realised that he can't drift through life always and has gone off and got himself a job.'

'But if he had, why disappear? He knew that was what I wanted.'

'What *you* wanted?' Her voice showed her surprise. 'But Tommy said . . .'

'Tommy doesn't always tell the truth. He can twist anything to suit himself. When he told me he'd need more money because he was getting married, I told him he wouldn't get another penny and he stormed off in a temper.'

'I didn't know . . .' she began.

'Look, Elaine,' Garvin sounded tired, something he rarely did, 'let's stop this nonsense. Of course you know where Tommy is. And you're going to tell me.'

'I don't know. I keep telling you that I don't know where he is,' Elaine said angrily.

Garvin leaned back in his chair and folded his arms. 'Okay, if that's the way you want to play it . . . but I tell you one thing, you won't leave this island until I know where Tommy is.'

'What do you mean?' Elaine was startled. 'We've got to go back to the ship.'

'The ship has gone. If you tell me where Tommy is, the schooner will follow it with us on board, but, as I said before and I say it again, you don't leave this island until you tell me where Tommy is.'

Elaine was on her feet, furious. 'How dare you do this? We've got to go back. The dancing . . .'

'Dirk and his partner are on board. I arranged for that to happen as I knew you'd be a hard nut to crack.'

'A hard nut?' She couldn't speak for a moment. 'How dare you do this? I don't believe it. That ship can't have gone!'

She turned and ran, nearly stumbling over roots that went under the path as she made her way back down to the beach. She knew Garvin was following her, but he made no attempt to catch up with her, which was more frightening than ever.

Getting to the beach, the lagoon and the sea beyond it stretched away. She could see the liner. Far, far away . . . It had gone!

Standing very still, she took a deep breath. So now what? Alone with an angry man on an isolated island with no means of escape? The schooners had all vanished, there was no one in sight, not even a small boat. What was she to do?

'Well? Satisfied?' Garvin sounded amused

as he caught hold of her and swung her round. 'Are you going to tell me?'

'How can I when I don't know?' she shouted at him, trying to free herself from his hands.

'How do I know that you don't know?'

'Look . . .' She swallowed, for suddenly she was afraid. There was a strange look in his eyes and they were alone. Alone on an isolated island.

CHAPTER SIX

Elaine was frightened yet, at the same time, unsure whether she should be as she looked round the lonely countryside and wondered what she could do now Garvin had left her. How quiet it was! Not a human being in sight; indeed, not even an animal. Not a sound except the distant roar of the breaking of the waves on the rocks outside the lagoon.

It was then she had another shock, for she noticed two large suitcases on the ground at the end of the jetty. Her suitcases!

What on earth were they doing there? Then she saw her shoulder-bag in which she kept her passport, health certificate and also birth certificate in case it should ever be needed by their side.

How did they get on the jetty? They hadn't been on the small schooner that had brought

Garvin and herself to the island. Another schooner must have brought the luggage later. But why? With another shock, she realised what that meant: it meant that Garvin had planned it all, that he had meant to keep her here at his mercy.

A lump seemed to rise in her throat and she bit her lower lip to keep control as she told herself not to be so melodramatic; as her mother would have said, 'You've been watching the telly too much and let your imagination carry you away.'

Garvin wasn't like that, Elaine told herself firmly. But wasn't he? Didn't this prove it? Why hadn't he told her what he wanted to know, why go to all this trouble to have her alone? And why did he want her alone?

She shivered suddenly though the wind was warm and the sunshine hot. Did this mean it had nothing to do with Tommy? Had Garvin some frightening desire to have her alone and helplessly at his mercy?

Surely, not . . . surely she knew him better than that. But did she? Apart from their dancing times and then when they discussed their dancing, she knew nothing at all about him—except what Tommy had told her, and that, so she now knew, hadn't always been true, and from what Fiona had said, and the Morrises, too. Elaine herself, she realised, knew very little about Garvin. And what had Mike called Garvin? A womaniser.

Had he been certain she would tell him where Tommy was? Was that when Garvin had decided to frighten her? And succeeded. Which was absurd, yet she knew she could not help believing it. Real fear seemed to swamp her. Never had she felt so helpless, so shocked. What could she do? This man she loved . . .

Her thoughts jerked to a standstill. The man she loved? But how could she love him? Certainly she enjoyed dancing with him and talking to him, but that couldn't mean *love*.

Or could it?

How happy she had been, how grateful to him for bringing her to this unknown island when all the time . . . Suddenly she found herself laughing, a wild hysterical kind of laughter she had never given before. Nor could she stop—though she did abruptly when she heard Garvin's voice:

'Come on,' he was shouting. 'Breakfast is cooking!'

She looked up and saw him come down the path with his long graceful stride that seemed to carry him effortlessly over the ground.

Staring at him, she wondered what she should do. What could she do? Stand here alone for ever, staring at the empty sea, completely cut off from the world? What would happen to her? Where could she sleep —what could she eat?

She wouldn't be missed until the liner got back to England, then her mother would go to the police. Would they ask the liner's passengers and crew and eventually find the island? Would she still be here? Or only her body . . . She started to laugh again, the wild hysterical laugh that was impossible to stop . . .

This time it stopped because of the smarting smack of Garvin's hand on her cheek that made her choke but stop laughing.

'What the hell's the matter with you?' he asked angrily. 'You sounded like a monkey or a drunken witch!'

'I . . . I . . .' she gasped, pressing her hand against her sore cheek.

'I'm hungry,' he said, but she didn't hear his words, for she was staring at this strange frightening Garvin. His face seemed to have changed, his mouth was a thin compressed line, his eyebrows close, his eyes narrowed, his voice cold.

She turned and ran . . . but he was too quick and in a few strides had caught up with her.

'Stop playing the fool!' he shouted as he grabbed her in his arms, holding her tight so that her body was pressed against his. 'What's the matter with you? I go to the trouble to cook you a decent breakfast and this is all the thanks I get!' He looked down at her pale face and saw her fear-stricken eyes and let her go so abruptly she nearly fell over.

'What the hell are you thinking?' he asked,

his voice deep and cold. 'Are you afraid I'm going to either murder or rape you?'

She couldn't answer as she stared miserably at him, for those fears had been hers. This was a stranger, not the friendly dancer she had known and liked so much—and she was completely at his mercy.

Garvin burst out laughing. 'Good grief, you must be out of your mind! I've got better things to do than that. Come and have breakfast. I'd better hurry or the bacon will be burned. You know the way?'

Dazed, she nodded, and he left her, turning to say: 'You will come, won't you? We haven't got much time to spare. I've phoned for a car, but we must eat first.'

She followed him, but he was soon out of sight, lost among the palm trees and dominated the scene. She walked slowly, for each step was an effort. She just couldn't understand it. He could change so swiftly—his violence and then cooking breakfast, her luggage—and now phoning for a car. None of it made sense. Or did it, for what was it he had said:

'I've better things to do . . .' when he talked of murder or raping her. Now had she been Felicity . . . ?

Finally Elaine reached the hut. She knew she had no choice in what she was doing, for he would only follow her and force her to do what he said. Even if she fought him, he was

too strong, and if she made him furious . . .
Somehow she must behave as if nothing had
happened—yet she felt an almost irresistible
desire to turn and run away, for she had a
strong feeling that knowing Garvin could only
mean pain.

He came out of the hut. 'Breakfast is ready.
Sorry everything is rather chaotic.'

It wasn't. She was startled inside the hut, for
the room, though small, was tidy with white
walls and brightly coloured paintings and red
curtains on the small window. He touched the
silk and smiled.

'One of my mistakes. I told Marge I liked
red once and she made the curtains. I must
have been daft, because I hate the colour, but I
haven't the heart to tell her so.'

The small table with two chairs was laid
with a white cloth, bright red plates covered
with sausages, bacon and fried eggs. There was
toast and marmalade as well as butter and
large red mugs for the coffee.

'You seem to have a lot of red,' Elaine
managed to say, keeping her voice steady.

He laughed. 'Marge's do, I'm afraid. I think
it's ghastly.'

'I like it,' Elaine told him. 'A warm colour.'

'I prefer cold colours. Take sugar?' He was
pouring the coffee as he spoke.

'Thank you.'

'I'm hungry, aren't you?'

'I don't know.' Elaine stared at the crowded

69

plate before her.

'Well, eat up. The car will be here in twenty minutes.'

She looked at him. 'I don't understand . . .'

'Neither do I.' His face was grave. 'Why were you so frightened of me? I'd have thought you'd have known me by now.'

'I couldn't understand why my . . . my luggage was there.'

'Your luggage? Oh yes. I asked the steward to pack it and a later schooner brought it out.'

'But why?'

He poured out a second cup of coffee: his plate was empty, though hers was still half full.

'You'll know in an hour,' he said, his voice grim. 'Now eat up, there's a good girl.'

'Did you cook it?'

'Who else? I always keep a fridge full of food here.'

'Is it your home?' Even as she spoke, Elaine looked round, seeing a bookcase of paperbacks, a small desk and a leather armchair that had one of those foot-rests that come up as the chair goes back a little. Yet it seemed an odd home for a man like Garvin.

He laughed. 'Hardly my home, just a hideout. Sometimes when I'm here, staying on the island, I get so fed up I feel I can't stand any more. I have no pretty girl convenient to dance with, so I come along here and brood. That's why the fridge is full. The funny thing is that the more I worry, the hungrier I get.'

'Do you worry?' she asked, then wished she hadn't, for his face changed for a moment as if a cloud had passed over it.

'Far too much,' he said, and stood up. 'We must go down to the jetty to get the car.'

Hesitating, Elaine looked at the dirty china. 'Shouldn't we . . .'

'Not on your life,' Garvin said, and laughed. 'Marge would never forgive me. She comes over every day to keep house for me, as she puts it. Come on.'

Who was Marge? Elaine wondered as she followed him. Some girl, young and dedicated to him, obviously. There must be many girls like that, in love with him.

The car was waiting by the jetty. Elaine saw that her luggage had vanished. It was no doubt in the boot of the car.

'I still don't understand—' she began, for her fear was vanishing, albeit slowly, but nevertheless she felt more at ease.

The chauffeur, a short stubby man with dark hair and skin, opened the car door for them. Garvin spoke to him in a language Elaine could not trace—partly Spanish, a little French and odd words of English. Once inside the car, Garvin turned to look at her. 'You will understand,' he said. 'You will.'

Was there a threat in his words? What did he mean? But he was obviously not in a talkative mood any longer as he sat, arms folded, head turned, face grim as he stared out

71

of the window.

She did, too, but was too puzzled and still a little dazed to really see anything. Vaguely she noticed that the part they had been in and that was so quiet and lonely was gradually vanishing as the car drove along the coast road and then up the road that wound round the hill, for everything changed. She saw cows, sheep and occasionally a dog. There were white houses, some way apart, but nevertheless they were houses! Mostly made of stone and hard to see as they were half hidden by great arches of creepers with their vivid purple and red flowers. All of the houses, when she could see well enough, had wide verandahs and beautiful gardens. There were several cars that passed and a few cyclists. It all changed even more as they approached a small town with a few stores and a garage. Farther on they came to a real town with skyscraper offices and huge blocks of flats and a wide pavement and road that ran by the sea, and the fairly large docks where several schooners were and also a few yachts anchored and swaying in the water.

It was so utterly different from the island on the other side. It was almost unbelievable.

'Well?' Garvin asked, his voice amused. 'Quite a change, eh?'

'I had no idea . . .'

'I thought you wouldn't.' The amusement had left his voice and he spoke dryly.

She drew a long deep breath. What a fool

72

she had been! Afraid of being alone on the island with him, when only a few miles away there were houses she could have run to . . . and asked for protection. What a fool she would have looked . . . if she'd been able to walk that far, of course. How she had exaggerated everything. How could she have been so stupid?

They drove through the modernised town and out to the country again. Here it was even more civilised with houses closer together and large gardens ablaze with flowers. She wondered how much farther they were to go— and where they were going in the end.

Finally the car turned off the main road and went down towards the sea far below, the water racing into the small sandy coves. After about ten minutes the chauffeur drove through an open iron gate towards a Gothic kind of house that seemed completely out of place, for it had four towers, and the house was square with wide windows and at least three stories and those strange long carved chimneys. The garden was perfect, bright with red carnations and large flowering shrubs and the usual purple-flowered creepers.

'Where are we?' she asked.

Garvin turned to look at her. 'This is where my wards live,' he said. 'Though I doubt if many are here at the moment. Tommy, for one.' His eyes were suddenly ablaze with anger. 'Why can't you tell me where he is?'

'Because I don't know!' she shouted back, then felt her cheeks go red as the chauffeur looked at her. She lowered her voice. 'I wish I could make you believe me. I don't know where Tommy is.'

'Is that so? We'll soon see about that!'

The front door opened and a woman stood there, an elderly woman with a slim figure and a bright pink silk dress, her white hair curly round her heart-shaped face, her eyes blue and eager as she came down the steps to meet them.

'Garvin, my darling,' she said quickly. 'You have found Tommy?'

He moved closer to her, taking her hands in his. 'Not yet, Aunt Rosemary. Not yet, I'm afraid, but I still have hopes.'

'Oh, Garvin . . . oh, Garvin . . .' Her face had changed, become haggard, that of a very old unhappy woman as the tears slid down her pale cheeks and she turned blindly away, feeling for the banister of the stone steps to help her up them before vanishing inside.

Garvin turned to Elaine, his face as made of stone. 'You understand now?' he asked.

CHAPTER SEVEN

Elaine stared at him, her nose prickling, her eyes filling with tears. 'Yes,' she said, 'I do understand.'

'Then tell me where Tommy is.'

'I don't know. Honestly, Garvin, I swear I don't know.' Her voice was desperately appealing. She put her hand on his arm. 'Now I understand—it's not only Tommy you're worried about, it's his grandmother. She looked so dreadful. The way her face changed, it aged, it . . . it was awful!' Her voice broke and she turned away, blinking her eyes in a vague attempt to hide the tears. She turned round. 'Garvin, you must believe me. I wouldn't have told you before, but now . . . now I've seen her and realise how much she loves Tommy, I'd do anything to help you find him.'

He stared at her. 'You know, I'm beginning to believe you. At the same time, it's a bitter disappointment. I was counting on you helping me.'

'I would if I could, but . . . Look, Garvin, Tommy was not my boy-friend. I hardly knew him—at least, not as a boy-friend. He and . . .' She paused, her hand going to her mouth as she stared at the man by her side. Should she tell him about Felicity? Oughtn't she to, because maybe he didn't know. 'He used to come to my mother's monthly dance and we would have a drink together when . . .' Again she paused just before she would have said *Felicity danced with someone else.* Then he would tell me all his problems.'

'Money?'

She nodded. 'Yes, he was always spending more money than he had got, but he never worried, because, he always said, his Uncle Garvin would help him out.'

'You don't know any of his friends?' Garvin began, then looked up at the sun blazing down. 'I'm sorry,' he said. 'Let's go inside.'

They went up the stone-white steps and into a cool hall. Elaine glanced round and saw on the walls large oil paintings of different people—probably the family. The tallboy was obviously a valuable antique and there were some lovely silver ornaments. She followed him through the hall and out at the back to a wide verandah. Straight ahead could be seen the sea, not so very far below, the long waves racing in, tossing up the foam, roaring gently. There were chairs and a table.

'Sit down, Elaine,' said Garvin, taking off his coat. He was wearing a pale pink shirt with his fawn-coloured suit. 'It is hot.' He rang a bell on the table and a tall, dark-haired elderly man came with a friendly smile. He, too, spoke in the strange language and Garvin answered him, then the elderly man turned to Elaine and bowed.

'We are happy to see you, mees,' he said slowly in English.

Elaine found herself bowing in return. 'Thank you. You are kind,' she said. He smiled and bowed to Garvin and left them.

Garvin was smiling. 'He's bringing us some

cold drinks. Now where were we? Oh yes, I was asking if you knew any of Tommy's friends. Maybe that could give us a clue.'

Elaine hesitated. Surely if he had found out that she knew Tommy, he would also have found out about Tommy's relationship with Felicity. If he didn't know, would he want to— for obviously Garvin had liked Felicity very much.

'Who did he take to the monthly dance?' Garvin asked.

Elaine took a deep breath and looked at him. 'Felicity.'

She was surprised when he smiled. 'I wondered how long it was going to take you to tell me that. Why didn't you on the ship?'

'Because I didn't want to help you find Tommy. I felt it was better for him to grow up and look after himself.'

'And now?'

'Now it's different. I want to help you find him.'

'Why is it different?' he asked as the elderly man brought out a tray of glasses, bottles and ice buckets. When he had gone, Garvin turned to Elaine. 'Why have you changed your mind?'

She twisted her hands together, looking at them, hoping he would not read between the lines of what she said. 'Because I know you and I realise that I was wrong. I thought you were an old man who was bored to tears with his ward and was generous with money in order to get rid of him.'

'You got that impression?' Garvin sounded amused.

She looked up. 'Yes, I did. I'm a great believer in ambition and independence, and it seemed to me that Tommy's life was being ruined by . . .'

'Me. Yet you didn't tell me at the hut. Was it seeing his grandmother?'

'Yes. I know now I was wrong, but I had a feeling that Tommy had no one to love him. I don't know why, but he never mentioned his granny or his brothers and sisters. He never said so, but I got the impression that he was an only child.'

'I can imagine. One of Tommy's weaknesses is that to him, there is only Tommy Brenton.'

'He thinks the world of Felicity. She's the one he spends all his money on. She's from a wealthy family and expects the best,' Elaine said, and stopped, suddenly remembering that Garvin himself was obviously in love with Felicity. In a wild hunt for something to cover her tactless remarks, she remembered something he had said: 'You said you wondered when I would tell you about Felicity. Did you know all along? Was that why . . .' she began, then stopped abruptly before she said too much.

'Yes, I did know. The private detective who traced you also traced her. But that wasn't why I devoted myself to Felicity on the ship. There were two reasons. If you're interested.'

'Yes, I am,' Elaine said eagerly, and felt her cheeks burn as she hastily looked away at the lovely sea. Had she betrayed the truth—the truth she now knew for sure. That she loved Garvin—as she had never loved before. But he mustn't know.

'Well, one reason was that she is, undoubtedly, very attractive indeed,' Garvin said slowly. 'Amusing, interesting to talk to—and the second reason was that for some reason or another she was chasing me.'

'Chasing you?' Elaine turned round, startled. 'But . . .'

'Well, I found out a few things. Maybe you know I'm one of the directors of the firm that built *Wonderland*—and apparently a pal of mine met Felicity a few days before we sailed and told her about me. Next day she put her name down for a last-minute cancellation which she got.' He laughed. 'So she got on the ship where I—a very eligible bachelor—would be.'

'You mean—you mean . . .'

'Yes, that's what I mean. Our beautiful attractive Felicity is looking for a wealthy husband. Did Tommy ever talk of marrying her?' Garvin's voice had changed, lost its light amusement.

'Never to me. But I think . . . I thought he loved her. Did you ask Felicity if she knew where Tommy was?'

79

'No. I knew at once that she couldn't help me.'

'Yet you thought I could.'

'Exactly. You and Felicity are totally different. You might be at either end of a long pole. I can't see Tommy weeping on Felicity's shoulder . . .'

'But you can on mine?'

He smiled. 'You're going to be a wonderful grandmother one day. A mixture of spoiling and serious advice. The only trouble with you is that you're always sure you're right.'

'I am?' She was startled, also rather dismayed. A good grandmother, he'd said. Who wanted at twenty-two to think of the days when she was a granny? Felicity was the beautiful attractive girl while she, Elaine, looked like being a good grandmother!

'Yes, you do,' he said gravely. 'What right had you to condemn me before you even knew me? What right had you to lay down the law and say I was spoiling the boy, being over-generous? Would you want me to have refused him help? It was a bad shock when his mother died, bad enough when he lost his father, but my sister spoiled him terribly. He was her first child and she never forgot it. When I took over the guardianship, I knew Tommy needed someone he could trust and rely on when he was in trouble. I admit I didn't think it would take so many years.'

'That's why I think that maybe it is a good

thing he has run away—to prove to himself and to you that he can manage alone,' said Elaine.

'But can he?' Garvin asked.

She frowned. 'How can he until he's tried?' she asked.

Garvin was smiling. 'You're so sure you're right, aren't you?'

Again, he made her blush. 'It's just . . . just the way I was brought up. My father thought the best gift you could give your child was to teach her to stand on her own feet.'

'Her? What about *him?*' Garvin asked with a smile.

'Her or him, then. After all, you never know when . . . when something is going to happen and the children have to . . . to be on their own.'

'That's true. I learned the hard way.'

'So Fiona, the hostess, said.'

They heard a noise and looked round. The old lady was coming to join them, her eyes a little red-rimmed, but she had a smile fixed determinedly on her face.

'Forgive me, my dear,' she said, smiling at Elaine. 'I find that as I grow older I become more emotional. Introduce me, Garvin darling.'

Garvin was on his feet, his voice tender as he helped her to a chair.

'This is Elaine Thomas, one of Tommy's friends. Elaine, my aunt, Lady Rosemary Brenton, Tommy's grandmother.'

They smiled at one another. 'So you know Tommy quite well?' Lady Rosemary asked eagerly.

'I'm afraid not quite well,' Elaine said. 'My mother has a dancing school and once a month has a dance and Tommy usually comes to it. That's how I got to know him.'

'You've no idea where he is?'

'I'm afraid not.'

'He didn't say he was going away?'

'No. Actually at that last dance, we hardly spoke to one another. I didn't even know where he lived,' Elaine admitted.

'He came alone?'

'Oh no, he always brought Felicity along.'

'Felicity?' Lady Rosemary looked quickly at Garvin. 'You know her?'

'Yes. She was on our ship.'

'On the ship?' Lady Rosemary looked puzzled. 'What was she doing there? I mean, surely if she was Tommy's friend, she could have helped you find where he was, so if he doesn't mind her telling you, why hasn't he written and told us himself?'

'A puzzle, Aunt Rosemary. What about a cold drink?' Garvin asked.

'Thank you, dear. And this young lady?' Lady Rosemary smiled at Elaine. 'Are you here to help us find that naughty child?'

'He's not a child, Lady Rosemary. He's a man,' Elaine said.

The old lady smiled. 'A pity he doesn't behave like one, then.'

'Maybe he's never had the chance,' Elaine

said as Garvin filled her glass again with the delightfully cold drink.

Garvin laughed. 'Elaine has an idea that we've all spoilt Tommy—handled him the wrong way.'

The old lady smiled ruefully. 'I agree he has been handled the wrong way, but it was not *our* fault. It was before our time. You see, dear, he was my daughter-in-law's first child and she was so thrilled that she never forgot it. She had six children, but Tommy was, to her mind, the sweetest. Fond as I am of Tommy, I wouldn't say that, but his mother did. Not only was he his father's favourite, for my son, like most men, badly wanted a son, but he was also his mother's favourite. He always got what he wanted and when he wanted it. He adored his mother and when she died, so soon after his father's death, it was terrible. He changed completely,' the old lady went on, holding her glass in her hands, her voice sad. 'He receded, just went dumb. He wouldn't eat, wouldn't speak to anyone, just sat, staring into space. He'd always been supported and now there was no one to hold him up. That's where my darling Garvin came in . . .' She looked at him and smiled, a sweetly loving smile. 'He was wonderful, really wonderful. That's why Tommy thinks so much of him.' Her face clouded again. 'That's why I'm so frightened, my dear. Surely he must realise how worried we'll be without any news of him. I can't understand it at all,' she sighed.

'Elaine, would you say Tommy was on drugs?' Garvin asked.

'Goodness, no!' Elaine said at once. 'We often discussed it. He was as much against it as I am.'

The old lady smiled. 'That's one of the things I was afraid of.'

'I'm sure you needn't be, Lady Rosemary,' Elaine said earnestly. 'Tommy isn't like that. He doesn't smoke much either.'

'Then what is your opinion? Why has he just vanished like this?' the old lady asked anxiously.

Elaine hesitated, looked at Garvin, who smiled. 'She knows, Elaine,' he said. 'I mean that I told Tommy he was far too young to get married and that if that was his idea, he'd better get a job.'

'That's what I think he's doing,' Elaine said quickly, leaning forward as she looked at the anxious, sad old lady. 'I think Tommy is finding himself a job and that as soon as he's got it, he'll get in touch with you. He's got to prove that he can do it.'

Lady Rosemary looked relieved. 'You could be right, my dear.' She looked at Garvin. 'Maybe we're making a fuss about nothing.'

'Maybe we are,' Garvin agreed. 'Which room can Elaine have, Aunt Rosemary?'

'The pale pink one,' said the old lady, smiling at Elaine. 'That's the one with the right colour for her lovely hair and it has the best view. You like looking at the sea?'

'I love it,' smiled Elaine.

'Good—then I must show you my studio and workroom and . . .'

'Aunt Rosemary is a woman of many talents,' Garvin said with a smile. 'She's a famous artist.'

'Not famous, dear boy,' Lady Rosemary said quickly, with her cheeks going pink.

'Well, look at the price you get for them. My aunt paints these pictures, Elaine, sells them and gives the money to her favourite charities, usually children and old people. She also does some sculpture work and knits and crochets. I've never known anyone work so hard, and she's no chicken, are you, Aunt Rosemary?' he said with a warm tender smile.

Elaine felt a slight pain. If only he would look at her like that, she thought.

Lady Rosemary laughed. 'Well, it's a long day when you have no housework or shopping to do and now the children are all away or at school, so I need plenty of interests. I certainly am no chicken,' she added with a smile. 'I'm eighty-six.'

'You're not?' Elaine was startled. 'Eighty-six? You don't look it.'

'I don't feel it either,' Lady Rosemary said with a smile that quickly vanished. 'Except sometimes.'

'Well, we all feel like that sometimes, don't

we, Elaine?' Garvin asked.

'We certainly do,' Elaine agreed.

Lady Rosemary laughed. 'I can't imagine you feeling old, my dear. What age are you? Sixteen?'

Garvin burst out laughing. 'Now she will be mad, Aunt. She's all of twenty-two and proud of it.'

'Do I look so young?' Elaine asked the old lady.

'You do, my dear. You have such a clear good skin, such lovely hair, such bright eyes.' Lady Rosemary looked up at Garvin, who had stood up. 'Aren't I right, Garvin?'

He smiled. 'You always are, Aunt Rosemary. Now, may I show her to her room? It's been a tiring morning and I guess Elaine would like a shower and change her dress.' He looked with some amusement at her yellow work dress.

She looked down at it. It was crumpled and awful-looking. 'I wanted to change,' she said quickly.

'There wasn't time.'

She was on her feet now. 'There could have been time. You just wanted . . .' She gulped down the angry words, suddenly remembering that the old lady was with them, looking puzzled. 'Yes,' Elaine went on, her voice calm, 'I would love a shower. It's very hot today.'

Elaine's bedroom was beautiful with pale pink silk curtains on the windows that gave a gorgeous view of the sloping garden, that went down towards the little cove where the sea was pounding in merrily, tossing the froth high. The bedspread was pink, the carpet pink. There was a large wardrobe and a big dressing-table.

'All very antique,' Garvin said. 'But Aunt Rosemary has been here for sixty years. She and her husband came here, sent for their furniture and have never changed it.'

'She's wonderful.'

'You haven't seen anything yet. She's amazing. I can't understand her. Do you know, she's lived here for sixty years and never left the island? She stayed here during both wars and, fortunately, the island didn't suffer much, nor was it of any geographical importance, but . . .'

Elaine stared at him. 'You mean she's never been off the island for sixty years? How awful!'

'She doesn't think so. It's full of memories for her. A happy marriage, several children, a busy life, then the children left home and her husband died. She chose to stay on. She had plenty of money, the house she loved, a staff of servants who loved her, work she enjoyed— and then, when my sister died, she took over the children.'

'Yet you were made their guardian?'

'I think my sister was worried because of Aunt Rosemary's age. Also she has no idea how to handle money.'

'And you have?' Elaine could not resist saying.

'I've had no choice. My sister left me all the money she had inherited from her husband. So I kept one third in the bank for emergencies and had the rest divided in six so each one has the same trust allowance when he or she comes to a certain age. So far it's only Tommy and Julia. She's just twenty-one and is married. Pete who's eighteen will get his trust allowance in two years' time. He's away at school in England. Luke who is sixteen is with him. They come back here for holidays—they love it. Emily and Patricia go to school here, though Aunt Rosemary and I are seriously thinking of sending them to a good boarding school in England or Switzerland. They're nice kids. You'll meet them. Well, have your shower, change into something you feel happier in.' He was looking amused as he spoke. 'Trews are allowed. Aunt Rosemary is well trained and quite trendy in her views. Then come down. I know Aunt Rosemary is longing to show you her hobbies. They really are good.'

He left her and she went to stand on the small balcony, gazing down at the garden full of bright red flowers as well as yellow, white and purple. The colour was gorgeous, the sea beautiful, the cloudless blue sky lovely . . . Elaine drew a long deep breath. Everything was so lovely . . . yet such a short time ago she had been frightened, so convinced that Garvin had some terrible plan . . . How could she have thought that of him? How could she?

Later, in her white trews and a thin green top, she went downstairs. Lady Rosemary was in the hall, looking at some books.

'Come along, my dear,' she called. 'Feeling better? Garvin can be so exhausting.'

Elaine was startled. 'I . . . I don't . . .'

'Understand?' the old lady laughed. 'I mean the way he teases one.'

'Oh yes, he does,' Elaine laughed.

Together they went through the large studio and Elaine saw some beautiful paintings and some small but lovely sculptures.

'You are clever,' she said admiringly.

Lady Rosemary laughed. 'When you live in a place like this, you need work you love. I enjoy this sort of thing and it keeps me busy. Never a dull moment on Paradise Island.'

'You've been here so long. Don't you want to . . . well, to see the world?'

'The world? What sort of world is it today, my dear? I listen to the radio and it breaks my heart to hear of the cruelty, the wickedness, the terrible things that are happening in the world today. Here on this island we live in peace and on good terms with each other. No, I don't want to go out in that horrible world. I'm happy here.'

'It certainly is very lovely,' Elaine agreed.

'I'm glad you like it, my dear. Now let's go and have a cold drink in the garden and tell me about your life. Garvin says you're a very fine dancer. He said it was a pleasure to dance with you.'

'He did?' Elaine's surprise made her speak eagerly and she looked at the old lady rather worriedly in case the eagerness had betrayed the truth—but it didn't seem to, for Lady Rosemary went on:

'Garvin is a mass of contradictions. He can be hard and stern and the next moment soft and anxious as any hen looking for a missing chick. You can imagine the shock he had when at the age of twenty-four, he found himself guardian to six children. He takes his responsibilities very seriously. He's been terribly worried about Tommy. You don't—somehow?' The old lady looked at Elaine.

Twisting her hands as she always did when not sure what to say, Elaine frowned. 'Honestly, I think Tommy is quite able to look after himself. Maybe he was annoyed when Garvin told him he was too young to marry and that he must learn to stand on his own legs and earn a living before he got married—well, isn't that the sort of thing that always makes children defiant and determined to prove what they can do? There's a childish streak in Tommy.' Elaine smiled. 'Maybe that's why we're so fond of him, but there must always come a time when a child becomes a man.'

'And that's what you think has happened? What a comforting girl you are, Elaine! You could be right, you know, and we are fussing over nothing. If only he would just send us a postcard. Young people are so selfish.'

'I'd say *thoughtless*,' Elaine said quickly. 'I think being selfish is doing something when you know it will hurt someone—I don't think Tommy would want to hurt you, but he might be so engrossed in finding a job that he doesn't think.'

Lady Rosemary patted Elaine's hand. 'You're a sweet girl, my dear. I suppose we must just wait and see.'

That afternoon Emily who was fourteen and Patricia only twelve years old came home from school. When both saw Garvin there were cries of delight.

'Uncle Garvin! Uncle Garvin, you didn't let us know you were coming.'

Both were tall slender girls with red hair and green eyes—both obviously adored Uncle Garvin. And he, just as obviously, adored them.

The next few days were very pleasant. Garvin was in a good mood, making Aunt Rosemary laugh a lot, cheering her up, Elaine thought. *Lady* Rosemary was most friendly, too, making Elaine feel welcome though she often wondered why she was there. Had Garvin really thought she knew more about Tommy than she did?

Lady Rosemary was always talking about Tommy and how wonderful his Uncle Garvin had been.

'There was poor Tommy who seemed to have retreated into himself after his mother died,' Lady Rosemary told Elaine one day. 'Garvin tried to replace the security the boy had lost and encouraged him to meet people, to stop sitting alone, staring miserably into space. He encouraged Tommy to paint and arranged for him to go to Paris, Rome and Greece to have lessons. To see the world—as Garvin said. Unfortunately Tommy got mixed up with the wrong kind of people and spent far too much money.'

That was largely Felicity's fault, Elaine was thinking, but decided it was wiser not to say anything about Felicity, for it was obvious that, despite what Garvin had said about Felicity looking for a wealthy husband, he had more than liked her.

Oddly enough, Elaine was thinking of this in the garden when she heard a car drive up. As she wondered who it could be, for both Lady Rosemary and Garvin were sitting with her, drinking cold drinks, they heard a voice—a voice both Elaine and Garvin recognised.

His face changed quickly—became amused, then interested as he turned to hurry into the house.

'I wonder who that is,' said Lady Rosemary. 'I'm not expecting any visitors.'

Well, she had got one, Elaine thought, as Garvin came back, smiling, with Felicity close behind.

CHAPTER EIGHT

'Felicity!' Garvin exclaimed. She stood there smiling, as usual elegantly dressed in her coffee-coloured trouser suit, her blonde hair beautifully done, her eyes amused as she looked at Elaine.

'This is a surprise,' Garvin said after he had introduced Felicity to Lady Rosemary, who was sitting very still, her face puzzled as she stared at Felicity.

'I suppose it is.' Felicity had sat down, accepted a long cold drink, and now looked amused. 'You know, Garvin, you never made me realise just how worried you were about your nephew. I knew Tommy had disappeared, but then men often do that—go off on a holiday and forget to let their family and friends know. Then when you and . . .' she paused and looked at Elaine, 'came to the island I realised just how very worried you must be. Fortunately the liner was stopping at various places on the African coast, so I got off at the first one with an airport, and here I am.'

Garvin was smiling. 'So I see. Might I ask why?'

She smiled at him. 'I've just told you—I've come to see if I can help you in your search for Tommy.'

Lady Rosemary's face brightened as she

leaned forward. 'You know where he is?' she asked eagerly.

'I'm afraid not,' said Felicity, turning to the old lady. 'But I do know the clubs he belongs to and the names and addresses of his friends.' She looked at Elaine. 'I don't think you can be of much help,' she said contemptuously. 'You hardly knew him.'

'That's what I said,' Elaine answered. How nasty Felicity made it sound—as if Elaine had pretended to know more about Tommy than she actually did.

'By the way,' Felicity went on, looking at Elaine with narrowed eyes. 'Mike was very hurt and upset when you vanished from the ship. You'd promised to go to the postponed audition when you got back to England and then you go off like that. He's got it all fixed up and now he has to find a girl to take your place. He couldn't understand what made you leave the ship, because, he said, you were so keen on the audition and had begged him to arrange it.'

Elaine drew a long deep breath as she clenched her hands, fighting down the anger that filled her. What a lot of lies!

She tried to keep her voice calm as she answered: 'That isn't true. There was never any suggestion of a, second audition.'

'He told me that,' Felicity said indignantly.

'I'm not saying he didn't tell you—what I am saying is that it's not true. He hardly spoke

94

to me on the ship, and when I told him I couldn't attend the audition, he was furious with me. There was never any question of a second one. At the time, I wished there had been.'

'You didn't mention it to me,' Garvin joined in.

'No, I didn't—because there was never any suggestion that he could arrange another audition.'

Lady Rosemary leaned forward. 'You know many of Tommy's friends?'

Felicity turned to her. 'Oh yes, I knew Tommy well, very well. I hope I can help you. You must be very worried. Tommy is so young and immature, but also—' she smiled with her enchanting smile directed towards Garvin, 'a darling,' Felicity finished.

'He never hinted that he planned to go away?' Garvin asked.

'No—not really. We had a quarrel, but then we often did. Tommy demanded what he wanted and expected to get it. He could never understand why I couldn't always go out with him. The last time I saw him, he seemed on edge—as if he wasn't sure what he was going to do. I asked him to come down to stay with my parents for the weekend, which he often did—but he said he couldn't. I was surprised, as usually he jumped at the invitation. He didn't say *why* he couldn't come, though. I went home and stayed there for a week and when I got back to London, Tommy had vanished.'

'How did you know?' Garvin asked.

'I met his friends and we all wondered where Tommy was. Then the news was in the paper. I thought he'd come out here to see his grandmother. He thought the world of you,' Felicity added, smiling at Lady Rosemary.

'Dear boy,' the old lady sighed. 'I am so worried about him. Elaine here doesn't think we need.'

Felicity looked scornfully at Elaine. 'She hardly knows him. Where does she think he is?'

'She says she has no idea,' said Garvin.

'You don't know, do you, Elaine?' Felicity asked.

Elaine shook her head. 'I think Tommy is trying to get himself a job and . . .'

'That'll be the day,' Felicity said scornfully. 'What sort of work can he do? Painting and writing poetry!'

'Then what do you think he's doing?' Elaine asked, feeling the anger growing in her.

'Haven't a clue, but we'll find one, won't we, Garvin?' Felicity said with a smile. 'If we go through the list of his clubs and friends.'

Garvin stood up. 'I'd better show you to your room, Felicity,' he said. 'Then if you'll come down to the library, I'll make a note of those friends and clubs he belonged to. We know so little about Tommy,' he added as

Felicity followed him.

There was silence for a moment. Elaine gazed blindly at the lovely scarlet flowers. Felicity had turned up for one reason—to get Garvin. He had admitted that that was what she was after, yet he was so nice to her, and just before he had said, 'We know so little about him', meaning Tommy—yet how was that true? Hadn't there been a private detective? If that man had traced both Elaine and Felicity, then without doubt he must have found out what clubs Tommy belonged to and the names of his friends.

'Elaine . . .' Lady Rosemary's anxious voice broke up Elaine's thoughts, so she turned quickly. 'Do you think she can help us?' the old lady asked.

'Honestly I don't know. They were very good friends. I know he spent a lot of time with her.'

'He was in love with her?'

Elaine hesitated. 'Again, honestly I don't know.'

'My dear girl, you don't seem to know anything,' Lady Rosemary said, her voice slightly accusing, slightly amused.

'I know I don't. I keep telling Garvin that. I don't know why . . .' Elaine stopped speaking abruptly, wondering just how much the old lady did know. Had she any idea that her beloved nephew had literally kidnapped her, giving her no chance to say she didn't want to

97

come and could not help to find Tommy?

The old lady looked at her thoughtfully. 'I think he wants to try everyone to find the boy.'

Impulsively Elaine put her hand on Lady Rosemary's wrinkled ann.

'Please try not to worry. I'm sure Tommy is all right. I think he's looking for a job to prove to Garvin that he can manage on his own.'

'But that's so unlike Tommy. He's always been dependent on someone.'

'Then isn't it time he became independent? I think Garvin's remarks about marriage must have hit him, perhaps jerked him to the truth, that he wasn't fit to marry and . . .'

'But who did he want to marry, Elaine? Was it you?'

Elaine shook her head, her cloud of fair hair swinging. 'No, it wasn't me. There never was any question of it. We danced together, talked to one another when Tommy hadn't a partner.'

'What did you talk about?' Garvin asked as he joined them, startling Elaine, making her look round quickly and then be afraid lest he saw the truth in her eyes—that she loved him more than she ever thought it possible to love.

'Films we'd seen—people we'd met. The cost of living . . .' Elaine smiled. 'I once had a small flat and I knew Tommy had an expensive service flat, so as I told him, he must expect the cost of living to be high. At least doing my own cooking helped me to keep the cost down.'

'Nothing very intellectual,' Garvin said dryly. Elaine looked at him. 'Who's intellectual in a discothèque? Who wants to be?'

'He talked about us?' the old lady asked.

Elaine hesitated. She didn't want to hurt Lady Rosemary's feelings, yet Tommy had never once mentioned his grandmother. 'Oh yes, a lot,' she said. 'And he was always saying how generous Garvin was.' It was half the truth, surely that was better than making Lady Rosemary feel hurt?

The old lady smiled happily, but Garvin gave Elaine an odd look as if to say she was a liar and perhaps added the words 'as usual'.

Why, she asked herself, did she love a man who neither trusted or liked her—though he had seemed to in those happy days on the ship when they danced so much.

*   *   *

The days passed and Elaine's unhappiness grew. It worried her terribly to see the agony on the old lady's face—it hurt her equally terribly to see how fascinated by Felicity Garvin was. Perhaps what hurt most was the change in Lady Rosemary. Not that she showed it, but little hints made Elaine realise that Felicity had convinced the old lady that Elaine was a 'no-good'. Lady Rosemary still talked to Elaine, but there was a stiffness, a kind of chill in the way the old lady looked at

Elaine. Now there were two who preferred Felicity: Garvin and Lady Rosemary, Elaine thought miserably.

One day Felicity was with the old lady, admiring her paintings, and Elaine was walking round the garden thinking how lovely it was, when Garvin joined her.

'What are you looking so miserable about?' he asked.

She was startled. 'Am I?' As she looked up at the tall blond-haired man by her side, her hands ached to stroke his cheek, her arms ached to go round his neck, her mouth . . . Oh, it was just plain stupid of her, she thought miserably, to let herself fall in love with such a man. A man accustomed to beautiful, intelligent girls—not just a stupid dancer with no good looks at all.

'You are,' he said, 'getting bored here?'

'Bored? Why, no, but . . .'

'But? Let me have no buts, Elaine. Why?'

She twisted her hands together as she looked round at the green grass, the palm trees with their long slender trunks bent in strange angles, the sea so blue, the sunshine.

'I'm not bored. It's beautiful here, but . . .'

'There we are again—"but". Tell me what's worrying you.'

'Well, it's . . .' She paused. Did she really want to go? Yet how long could she stay here under these circumstances?

'Go on.' He caught hold of her and gave her

a gentle shake.

The warmth of his fingers made it hard for her to think and when he let go of her arms, she felt cold and alone.

'Well?' Garvin asked, sounding annoyed.

'It's just that I feel . . . well, I don't know what good I'm doing here. I mean . . .'

'You are doing a lot of good here,' he said, surprising her.

'But how? I know so little about Tommy.'

'Yet you believe in him. That comforted his grandmother. Also you keep her company when Felicity and I are phoning different addresses in England.'

Were they? Elaine wondered, for Garvin and Felicity spent hours alone together. Surely it couldn't take that long to phone?

'You want to go?' he asked.

She hesitated. Wouldn't it be better to go thousands of miles away from a man you loved without the slightest hope that he might love you? There could only be pain and sorrow here for her . . . yet to leave him—that thought, too, was unbearable she knew.

'No, I don't,' she said.

He smiled. 'Good. I'll let you know when you're redundant,' he said, and walked away.

She stood very still, staring at his back as he walked so fast, so gracefully.

Redundant, he had said.

CHAPTER NINE

It was a few days later that the surprise came. Three unhappy days for Elaine who could not forget the word *redundant*. Was that how Garvin saw her? *Something* that was still useful, but when she ceased to be, then . . . whang! out she could go. *Redundant* was an ugly word, even uglier when it described you and when the man who described you was the one you loved.

Felicity and Garvin seemed to be always busy; talking, phoning people—if that was what they were doing!—laughing together. Elaine felt left out, unwanted, *re* . . . She just stopped herself from thinking the word that haunted her. Lady Rosemary seemed glad to have her company, and yet here, too, Elaine felt that Lady Rosemary no longer liked or trusted their unwanted guest, Elaine Thomas.

Then the unexpected happened. They were sitting on the terrace in the shade. Lady Rosemary was knitting, her face tired with anxiety, while Garvin and Felicity were talking about someone they both knew in America and who had told Tommy that there was a chalet in Bermuda if he ever wanted to borrow it.

'It was colourful and popular for artists . . . but I can't see Tommy going there alone,'

Felicity was saying, while Elaine stared at the sea racing in, her hands twisted together, as she tried not to think of the hated word.

Suddenly there was the sound of a car—the sound of the front door bell—Pierre, the butler, whose surprised and delighted voice welcomed someone, and then footsteps down the hall, and the three people sitting down turned to stare in amazement as Tommy came striding towards them. He had long fair hair that curled on his shoulders, blue eyes and a sweet smile.

'Hi, folks!' he shouted as he walked fast. 'Here I am—at last!'

Felicity was first on her feet. 'Why, Tommy darling!' she exclaimed.

But Tommy walked past her, taking no notice at all as he made for his grandmother. Close behind him was a pretty girl with long dark hair tied back with a scarlet ribbon that matched her trouser suit.

She looked at Felicity who stood, still and startled. 'Hullo,' the stranger said. 'You must be Felicity, Tommy's old girl-friend. I've heard a lot about you,' she added with a smile.

'And who are you?' Felicity asked, her voice cold.

The girl laughed. 'Ask Tommy. He'll tell you.'

Tommy was in his grandmother's arms as the tears rolled down her cheeks slowly. 'My Tommy,' she kept saying. 'You're all right?'

He kissed her and wiped the tears away with a tissue the girl handed to him. 'I'm sorry to have upset you so, Gran,' he said. 'Jackie told me I should write to you, but I wanted us to be married before we saw you.'

'Married?' Lady Rosemary almost gasped. Tommy turned and put his arm round the girl by his side. 'Meet my wife, Gran—Jackie.'

'My dear!' Gran gasped.

Jackie smiled. 'I've heard so much about you,' she said, then she looked round and saw Garvin who was still standing silently, though Felicity had sat down. Elaine stood in the background, or so she thought, but Tommy turned to her.

'Hi, Elaine. This is a surprise.' He went to her and lightly kissed her on the cheek. 'What are you doing here? And what do you think of my bride?'

Before Elaine could speak, Garvin moved forward.

'It can't be true,' he said sarcastically. 'Why, she looks as if she's barely out of the schoolroom.'

Jackie laughed. 'They all say how young I look, but I'm twenty-two. You're right about the schoolroom, Uncle Garvin, but I happen to be the teacher.'

'You don't say!' Garvin looked startled.

Jackie turned to Tommy. 'Tell them about us, Tommy.'

Tommy laughed. 'What shall I tell them?

That we were married and flew straight out here—that we've got jobs in a school in Cornwall. I'm teaching Art while she teaches English, History and goodness knows what. She's a clever girl, is my Jackie.'

Jackie laughed, her face happy, her eyes sparkling. 'And you're a great artist. One day we'll both be famous, but there's no hurry. We've years ahead of us.'

'One day we're going to build our own house,' Tommy went on. 'I'm studying architecture in my spare time as we want it to express us, but we're not sure where. Actually we're on our way to Swaziland where we're going to have our honeymoon, but we wanted to drop by here first to tell you.'

Garvin was still standing, though Elaine, too, had sat down. He was looking sceptical and Jackie seemed to see it, for she turned to him.

'Don't worry, Uncle Garvin,' she said, her voice light yet with a subtle undercurrent of firmness. 'With what Tommy is going to earn and what I'll earn, plus his generous trust allowance, we won't be bothering you at all. We shall be completely independent, won't we?' She turned to Tommy.

'You bet we will,' he said, smiling. 'What about a nice cold drink, Gran? We can only stay a couple of days as we haven't got long.'

Lady Rosemary smiled. 'I'm glad you came, Tommy boy. Do sit down, Jackie. What an odd name for a pretty girl!'

Jackie laughed. 'I was christened Jacqueline, but what a mouthful!'

'Jacqueline, Jacqueline,' the old lady repeated slowly. 'It's beautiful.'

'And so is my Jackie,' Tommy said proudly. 'One day we'll start our family . . .' He paused as he saw the startled look on his grandmother's face. He smiled. 'I said one day, Gran. I'm going to call my first daughter Rosemary and my second Elaine.' He smiled at the silent Elaine.

'How does Jackie feel?' Elaine asked with a smile. Jackie looked an absolute darling and Elaine liked the way Jackie made Tommy do the talking and lead the conversation. Tommy had been treated as a child far too long, and obviously Jackie knew that.

Jackie smiled. 'What Tommy says goes.'

They all laughed.

'I'd say it's gone too long,' Felicity chimed in.

Looking at her, Jackie's thin dark eyebrows grew close together.

'Tommy's fault is his generosity. He doesn't know how to say no when asked for something. That's been his handicap.'

Felicity's cheeks went pink, then murmuring something she stood up and hurried into the house. Jackie turned to Tommy.

'I'm sorry, Tommy, I shouldn't have said that.'

106

He laughed, took hold of her hand and laid it against his cheek. 'You did quite right, Jackie. It's time someone told Felicity the truth. Well, Gran . . .' he turned to the silent Lady Rosemary, 'aren't you pleased that your errant little grandson has decided to grow up and become a man?'

As he finished speaking, Tommy looked at his uncle. Garvin put down his glass and frowned.

'How long have you known Jackie?' he asked.

'Two . . . no, three . . . how long, Jackie?' Tommy turned to the girl by his side.

'Two months, three weeks and four days,' Jackie said with a smile.

'Is that all?' Lady Rosemary sounded rather shocked.

Tommy laughed. 'We knew at once, didn't we, Jackie? I took one look at her and knew that life was only worth living if she was mine.'

Jackie laughed. 'I took one look at him and thought "Help!" as if I had ants. The first time I'd ever felt like that just from looking at a man.'

'We knew we were made for one another, but first I had to get a job.' Tommy looked at Garvin. 'You were quite right in what you said. I hadn't realised it before.'

'So Jackie was the girl when you said you were getting married. I thought it was Elaine.'

'Elaine?' Tommy sounded really surprised,

and Elaine had to laugh.

'I told you, Garvin, we were just friends. We met once a month.'

'You were a convenient shoulder to weep on,' Tommy said with a smile. 'I used to get very depressed, and you always showed me the bright side.'

'What were you depressed about, Tommy dear?' Lady Rosemary asked. 'You should have told us.'

He laughed. 'I told Uncle Garvin until he must have been fed to the teeth. I seemed to be drifting through life with no goal to work for, as Elaine used to say.' He smiled at her. 'You were right, you know, Elaine. Life has no meaning unless you're working for something. Now I've got a wife, and one day . . .' he paused and smiled at his grandmother, 'one day there'll be more of us for me to work for.'

Elaine looked quickly at Garvin, but he was smiling at Jackie, who was laughing a little.

Tommy stood up. 'Come on, Gran, and show me your paintings. I inherited it all from you, you know.'

Lady Rosemary laughed. 'I thought I got it from you, Tommy dear. I never painted a thing until you were sixteen.'

'Maybe not, but the talent was there, hidden from view,' Tommy said, helping the old lady to her feet. 'I can't wait to see your latest.'

There was a sudden silence as they left and Elaine, Garvin and Jackie were alone. Then

Jackie smiled at Elaine.

'We've a lot to thank you for,' Jackie said, then she turned to Garvin. 'I'm sorry, Uncle Garvin, if I seemed rude when I spoke to you earlier. You've been most kind and generous to Tommy, but it's time you stopped treating him as a child. He is a man and must be treated as such. We'll manage somehow on what we earn.'

Garvin leant forward. 'I agree, Jackie, but it has been a difficult time. He loved his mother so much and missed her so that I was trying to take her place. I see now I was wrong. Remember I'm still his guardian and will always be worried about his welfare, so promise me that if things go bad—and they can without it being your fault—such as a car accident and long illness or something— promise that you'll let me know. I've got money of his mother's put away for such emergencies. I'm glad he's met someone like you.'

Jackie laughed. 'I'm glad I met Tommy. I promise if things go wrong like that, I'll let you know, but until I do, don't worry. We'll manage. It'll be fun.' She laughed happily. 'I always see an obstacle as a challenge. Too easy a life isn't worth living.'

Garvin laughed. 'I see you view things differently from most people. I wish my sister had divided the money so that each child got the same and left me out.'

Her face suddenly serious, Jackie shook her head. 'I'm glad she didn't. Tommy wouldn't have had a penny now. He's so generous, always buying people presents.' She laughed. 'I have to watch what I say. If I look in a shop window and say that's a smashing dress, Tommy walks in and buys it for me. That's how his money has gone before, for . . .' She paused and then went on. 'His other girl-friends have wanted too much. He just can't say no when a girl asks for something, so as I said, I have to watch out.' She laughed. 'One day, when he's famous and we're very rich, I'll let him buy me everything I like.'

'Jackie, Jackie!' Tommy exclaimed, hurrying out to the terrace. 'Do come and see the painting Gran has done of me. It's absolutely super. I'm jealous as can be—she paints far better than I do.'

'Impossible, darling,' said Jackie, jumping up, hurrying to join him.

There was a stillness as Garvin and Elaine sat alone. Gradually everyone was leaving the terrace, she wondered if she would be the last.

Garvin startled her when he spoke. 'So you were right!'

'Right?'

He nodded. 'You said Tommy needed responsibility. He's got it now.'

'Jackie's a darling,' Elaine said quickly.

'I agree. I wasn't suggesting she isn't a darling. I think Tommy is a very lucky young man. She'll make a wonderful wife. I wonder what sort of husband he'll make.' Again Elaine sensed disapproval in his voice.

'I think he'll make a very good one. He certainly loves her,' she said at once, leaping as always to Tommy's defence.

'What do you mean by the word *love?*' Garvin asked.

She looked at him quickly, but he was serious—there was no amusement betrayed by his lips or sarcasm in his eyes.

'I . . .' she began.

'Have you ever been in love, Elaine?'

'I . . .' She swallowed. How easy it would be to tell him the truth—to let him know that she was hopelessly in love with him! How would he react? Laugh like mad, no doubt. See it as a great joke.

Redundant, he had said. How that word hurt!

'Have you?' she asked.

'Frankly I don't know. There's many a pretty girl I've enjoyed taking out, but the thought of spending the rest of my life with her—well, that's a different thing.'

'It must be difficult.'

'Difficult?' Garvin's voice rose a little. 'What must be difficult?'

She looked at him quickly and away again, afraid he might see in her eyes what she must not let him see.

'As you said, spending your life with

someone you hardly know.'

'They seem all right. Two months, three weeks and four days,' Garvin quoted, and laughed. 'What a joke!'

'I don't think it was,' Elaine said stiffly. 'It just shows how much she loves him.'

'Would you know exactly how long you'd loved the man you were going to marry?' Now Garvin was looking amused.

'I don't see why not.'

'I don't see why.'

'Perhaps that's because you don't know what love is,' Elaine said, getting a little uncomfortable as well as annoyed with the way he liked to tease her.

'You do?' Garvin said sharply.

She looked at him and he looked at her. For a moment it was a strange feeling for Elaine as their eyes seemed to cling together, sending a message that neither of them understood, so she jerked her eyes away.

'We're back to Square One,' she said, trying to make her voice light. 'I'm not sure if I have been in love, but . . . but I think so.'

'What made you think so?'

She swallowed nervously. It was getting as bad again as it had been in the beginning. 'Well, you feel so unhappy.'

'Unhappy? In love?' Garvin sounded shocked. 'But that's crazy. Love should make you happy.'

'I suppose so,' she said, her voice miserable.

This she noticed at once and tried to laugh. It wasn't much of a success, but she did her best. 'It would depend on whether the one you loved loved you,' she said, and stood up. 'I've got a headache. I think I'll lie down.'

'A good idea. You seem rather confused,' said Garvin. 'See you anon.'

'Yes,' she managed to say, then almost dived for the door leading to the hall. Fortunately no one was around, so she escaped to her room where she could sit down and cry.

It was stupid to cry, she told herself, but that didn't help. Nor did telling herself that this was happening to millions of people every day and that she was not unique in her misery, but she must just accept the fact that in Garvin's life, she might soon become *redundant.*

CHAPTER TEN

The two days passed quickly and when the newly married couple had left them, there seemed a cold atmosphere in the house. No more of Tommy's laughter or Jackie's happy voice—now it was Felicity talking, Garvin laughing while Elaine sat quietly and Lady Rosemary smiled or hummed softly as she knitted a pullover for her dear Tommy.

'Jackie is a nice girl,' Lady Rosemary said one day as they sat on the terrace. 'Don't you agree, Elaine?'

'A very nice girl,' Elaine agreed. 'Just what Tommy needed.'

'I don't agree,' said Felicity. 'Can you see Tommy as a schoolteacher? He won't stick that for long, and what sort of money can they earn?'

'Enough,' Elaine said quickly. 'According to both.'

'They don't know what they're talking about. Wait until they get the telephone and electricity bills start coming in and the rest,' Felicity said scornfully.

That's what you want to happen, Elaine thought angrily. You'd like Tommy to get into debt and have to come crawling to Garvin for help. Well, that wouldn't happen. Tommy wouldn't let it happen any more, that was for sure. Elaine hated Felicity and would have told her what she thought of her—but how could she with Lady Rosemary there? And it wasn't just jealousy, Elaine told herself. Felicity was malicious, she told lies, and yet she was always believed. It seemed incredible that Garvin who had admitted that Felicity was looking for a wealthy husband and, despite what Jackie had said and Tommy implied, still found her fascinating, believing everything she said. It could only be because he loved her.

During the next few days Lady Rosemary was restless. She admitted she missed Tommy, though she was happy he was so well, and she asked Elaine if she would like to see the island. They went in the car with Leo, the chauffeur, and Elaine saw the beautiful flowers, the exquisite white camellias, the purple bougainvillaea, the crimson hibiscus, as well as the lovely palm trees with their slender stems bent away from the wind and the small brightly coloured birds singing above the beautiful orchids.

'This is a lovely island,' Elaine sighed.

Lady Rosemary smiled. 'I love it. As I told you, I've lived here since I was married and I never want to leave it. I never shall,' she added.

'Why leave it if you're happy?'

'Exactly. That's just what I say. Happiness is so important, Elaine dear.'

'So important,' Elaine agreed, and was shocked by the bitterness in her voice.

The old lady looked at her as if puzzled. 'Happiness doesn't just come, my dear girl,' she said gently. 'Sometimes you have to make it.'

'How can you make happiness?'

'There are many ways, some of them painful. You have to learn to accept disappointments—to know that though dreams don't always come true, other doors will open and you'll find happiness there. Take Marge—she adores Garvin. Always has— positively worships him, and dreams that one day she'll be Mrs. Humfrey.'

'And she won't be?' Elaine asked, wondering what this Marge, that she had so often heard about but never met, would be like.

Lady Rosemary laughed. 'It's most unlikely. She's hardly Garvin's type.'

Elaine drew a deep breath, twisting her hands together as she spoke.

'What is Garvin's type?'

'It's hard to tell. At the moment it seems to be Felicity. She's very beautiful.'

'Very,' Elaine said miserably, then forced herself to laugh, for Lady Rosemary must never know that the possibly-redundant-at-any-moment-uninvited guest was madly in love with Garvin.

'As you grow older,' the old lady went on, 'you grow more philosophical about things. At your age, Elaine dear, a disappointment seems to you like the end of the world. At my age, though I might be sorry, I would still know that something else will turn up. As I said before, when one door closes another opens, and this second door often leads you to something far nicer than your dream.'

Elaine was glad that the car drew up at the house at that moment, for it stopped the conversation as she was finding it difficult not to tell Lady Rosemary the truth, and ask her what door could possibly open when you were fatally in love with a man like Garvin.

At dinner that evening, Lady Rosemary

surprised them all. She was smilling happily as she looked at Emily and Patricia who were chatting about something that had happened at school that afternoon.

'I'm so happy about Tommy that I would like to celebrate,' the old lady said. 'How about a party one evening?'

The two red-haired girls were delighted. 'A real party? We dine and dance and drink?' said Patricia.

Her grandmother smiled. 'You can dine and dance, but not drink.' She turned to Garvin. 'Don't you think it would be a good idea, Garvin? It seems a long time since I entertained anyone and it would be nice for my friends to meet Felicity—and you, too, Elaine,' Lady Rosemary went on, turning quickly to the quiet Elaine, but she spoke hastily as if she had nearly forgotten Elaine.

'Why not?' said Garvin. 'Sounds a good idea.'

So it was discussed and then the housekeeper consulted. A week later, a really big party was held. It was a beautiful evening with a full moon breaking up the darkness and making a silver pathway across the ocean. The house was ablaze with lights, decorated with flowers. The staff were enjoying it as much as the guests, with big smiles on their dark faces, as they laughed and chatted.

Lady Rosemary welcomed the guests in the hall, introducing Felicity, and Elaine, who stood back a little, feeling herself unwanted. Was she, she wondered, already redundant, for the old lady was in good health, happy and certainly not needing a companion to look aftor her. When would Garvin say it was time for the unwanted guest to go? She had written to her mother, explaining why she would not be home as expected and that she did not know just when she would be home again.

At Garvin's suggestion—or was it an order?—Elaine was wearing the gown with layers of soft net in the long skirt, every shade of pink from the palest right down to deepest crimson. The top had a halter neck. It was a beautiful dress and Lady Rosemary had said with a smile:

'Just your colour, my dear.'

Of course Elaine's dress was nothing when compared to Felicity's. Felicity was superb in a leaf-green voile dress with a deceptively straight long skirt that as she moved swung sideways, showing off her beautiful legs. The bodice was also halter-neck with a high waist decorated with embroidery. Patricia and Emily were jaunting about in their gay long dresses, their red hair swept up high on their heads to make them look much older and it did. Lady Rosemary herself looked gracious and years younger than she was in her long black skirt and white lace tunic, pearls on her ears and round her neck and a small diamond tiara in her white hair.

Garvin was here, there and everywhere, welcoming guests, showing them the lofty large ballroom that was so seldom used these days and the long dining room with trestle tables covered with food while the staff stood behind them, smiling and ready to serve.

It was all very old-fashioned, Elaine thought, yet there was something charming about the old house, the antique furniture, the silver ornaments and the family portraits on the walls. Everyone seemed happy, talking, laughing, eating or dancing. Except Elaine, who stood, half hidden in a corner, watching Lady Rosemary dancing slowly in the arms of a man with a moustache. The girls were dancing, too, thoroughly enjoying themselves. So was Felicity. Where was Garvin—and where was Marge? Was Marge, of whom she had heard so much yet never met, at this moment in Garvin's arms?

Elaine was surprised and ashamed at the jealousy that swamped her. She had been brought up to believe that jealousy was a sign of weakness, that you should trust, but surely, in this case it was different, for Garvin had never pretended to find her attractive. Suddenly she knew what Lady Rosemary's words had meant about another door opening when one closed. She knew she ought to leave the island just as soon as possible and start forgetting Garvin and looking for someone to take Garvin's place in her heart.

Even if it broke her heart to go. For it would certainly break her heart if she stayed and was invited for his wedding to Felicity. So which would be worse?

Elaine jumped as a hand closed round her wrist. She turned and it was Garvin.

'What are you doing here?' he asked. 'Why aren't you mixing?'

'Because . . .' She thought fast and went on: 'Because I don't know anyone.'

'You know me. I've been looking for you, and here you are, half hidden.'

She stared at him. Was he joking? But she saw that he wasn't.

'Come along,' he said, and as they walked to the ballroom, he went on:

'She wants us to dance.'

'She?' Elaine queried.

'Aunt Rosemary. She says Tommy told her how beautifully you dance, so she would love to see you—and she finds it hard to believe that I can dance, too, so we've got to show her. What do you say?'

'What do you?' Elaine asked as they reached the dance floor and she went into his arms.

'I'm all for it. I miss our dances.'

'So do I. They were fun.'

'Good. Now will you do the Spanish dance? Then we'll dance together. You've got the clothes?'

'Yes.'

'Good. We'll do the dancing in about an hour, so that should give you time to change.'

Was that a hint, she wondered, to get her to go to her room and not be a nuisance?

'That will be fine,' she managed to say.

They danced until the small local band stopped playing, Elaine with her eyes tightly shut, relaxed in the arms of the man she loved but who hardly knew she existed. If only he was holding her because he loved her . . . if only . . . The music had stopped for a few moments before she realised she was still in his arms, and she moved away quickly.

Garvin was laughing. 'You were half asleep.'

She blushed. 'I am a bit sleepy.'

'Well, go and relax. Wear the white dress with the gold front and frills with gold lace. You've got the castanets?'

'Yes.'

'Come down in forty minutes, then. You do your dance first and then we'll dance together.'

'All right,' she said, and hurried to her bedroom. It was just as if he didn't want her about the place.

In her room, she got out the dress and shoes and did her hair up high on her head. There was a white camellia in the room to go behind her ear. She had done the dance so often she was not nervous, yet when she went down to join Garvin she had an uncomfortable feeling that the audience would not be the encouraging friendly crowd it had been on the

121

ship. Nor was she going to enjoy dancing with Felicity watching her.

What made it worse was that as she went out on to the floor, she saw that Garvin was standing by Felicity's side, his arm round her shoulder.

CHAPTER ELEVEN

When the music began in the lovely Spanish rhythm, Elaine was surprised how well the small band played. Surely not so well if they had only just been asked? That meant Garvin had planned all this and told them to rehearse the music to be played. Was it Garvin then who wanted to dance?

She went on to the floor, moving with rhythm and pleasure as the music took possession of her. She half-closed her eyes, thinking of herself as a joyous spanish girl, twirling round with the gold lace frills of her skirt swinging and her castanets crackling as she waved her hands about. She forgot everything but the joy of interpreting the beauty of the music, and as the dance came to an end and the guests clapped and shouted: 'Olé' it took her a few moments to realise where she was—then she saw Lady Rosemary smiling while Emily and Patricia, by their grandmother's side, were clapping their hands vigorously. But then Elaine saw Garvin and Felicity, half turned away as if they hadn't bothered to look at her, and Garvin was laughing.

Somehow Elaine curtseyed and bowed and curtseyed and finally escaped to the hall, almost into Garvin's arms.

'Change into your other Spanish dress, Elaine,' he said curtly.

Had she danced badly? Why did he sound so annoyed?

'Don't you like this one?' she asked.

'It's all right, but the red and white goes better with my dark suit. I didn't realise it until Felicity pointed it out.'

Felicity! Trust her to interfere, Elaine thought angrily, but she managed to smile. 'Don't forget your crimson cummerbund. I'll go and change now.'

As she hurried to her room, she realised he had not said one single word about her dancing. Not that she done well or how badly she had danced. Probably he thought the latter, for Felicity could be trusted to look for and point out plenty of faults! But Garvin hadn't said a thing—he had been so completely uninterested.

Elaine changed into the other dress that was gay with its bright colours. But she didn't feel very gay herself as she made her way back to the ballroom.

Lady Rosemary came to her side. 'That was

beautiful, my dear girl,' she said with a warm smile. 'You certainly have talent.'

Patricia and Emily came to her side, too. 'Smashing,' said Emily. 'I'd like to dance like that.'

'I wouldn't mind,' said Patricia, her red hair shining in the bright light from the beautiful chandeliers above. 'Only it means a lot of work, doesn't it, Elaine?'

'Quite a lot, but if you enjoy it . . .'

'You obviously do, my dear,' Lady Rosemary said. 'I can't wait to see Garvin dance. Somehow it doesn't seem like him.'

Elaine laughed. 'The days have gone when male dancers were considered effeminate. Nowadays people realise the hard work involved. Actually Garvin's dancing is a hobby and a relaxation from the worries of the world, he told me once. Just like some men play golf, so Garvin likes to dance.'

'How does he dance?' Emily asked.

'Beautifully,' Elaine told her. 'Quite the best dancer I know.' Which was true, for Garvin danced even better than Dirk—for some unknown reason he was a natural dancer.

'His parents were fond of dancing, but his father was so different from Garvin,' Lady Rosemary said.

'Gran's crazy about Uncle Garvin,' Emily explained, her green eyes sparkling. 'He can do nothing wrong.'

'He never does!'

124

'Oh, Gran, what nonsense,' said Patricia, tucking her arm through the old lady's. 'None of us are perfect. Even he must be human and make mistakes some times.'

He was making one now, Elaine thought, though she said nothing, for Garvin believed every word Felicity said—even though he knew the kind of girl she was.

The music changed and became Spanish and the guests hurried to their seats. Garvin joined Elaine in his dark suit, bright red cummerbund, and a matching carnation in his lapel buttonhole.

'Well, are you ready?' he asked.

'I've been waiting,' she told him.

The drums rolled and Garvin took hold of her hand as he took her on the floor, and the Spanish music with its buoyancy, its aliveness, lovely rhythm and almost intoxicating charm despite its strange dignity, and Elaine forgot her misery as her body swayed and moved. And she went into his arms that were warm round her body, and then she felt icily cold as she danced away from him. For a while it was absolute bliss and she wished they could dance for ever—and then, quite suddenly, she sensed something. Garvin was dancing stiffly, forcing himself, not relaxed and enjoying every moment of it as he had done on the ship.

What was wrong? Was he bored? Eager to get back to his beloved Felicity? Or was it Marge who loved him so much and who must

125

surely be here—somewhere?

She looked up quickly and saw that he was staring across the room, smiling. Smiling—not at her. Oh dear me, no! Was he smiling at Felicity or Marge? Never mind who it was—it most certainly was not her!

Perhaps it was her bitter jealousy or her miserable acceptance of the fact that Garvin did not see her—but she stumbled, her feet in his way, and it took skill on both sides and quite a few moments for them to regain their balance and the beauty of their dance. But they did, and when it was over the guests shouted and clapped, but Elaine curtseyed while he bowed and they hurried off the floor. In the hall, Garvin caught hold of her arm.

'I want to talk to you, alone. Come outside,' he ordered, his fingers digging painfully into her flesh.

She went meekly, knowing she deserved the scolding she was going to get. She could have ruined the dance, tripped him up and perhaps injured one of them. He must be furious. It was an unforgivably clumsy mistake, the sort that an amateur might make, but never a professional.

Out in the garden they walked along the terrace, far from the distant roar of laughter and voices. There were a few lanterns hanging from the trees, but they gave little light. There was no one there and Garvin put both his hands on her arms and turned her to face him.

She braced herself, prepared to admit her folly and face his fury. What he said startled her, because it was unexpected.

'What's happened?' he said. 'Why do you hate me so much?'

She stared at him, unable to believe what she had heard.

'I . . . I don't . . .' she began, then stopped. How thankful she was they stood in the dark and could barely see each other's features If it had been light, Garvin would have seen the truth in her eyes that she loved him more than she had ever believed it was possible to love.

'Felicity says it's very obvious,' he told her.

That was the last straw. 'Felicity!' Elaine said scornfully. 'What does she know about me? You can't believe a word she says. She's a liar and . . .'

'Elaine, please! That's not a nice thing to say. You've changed so much. Even Aunt Rosemary notices it. Felicity is on your side. She told us the reason. We'd never thought of how this must be affecting your future. You must feel you're wasting your time here.'

'I never said that!'

'I didn't say you did. It was Felicity who had the good sense . . .'

Something seemed to snap inside Elaine. 'Felicity knows nothing about me at all. We've never been friends, never talked. How can she know what I want to do?'

Garvin laughed. 'What a little spitfire you

are! In a real bad mood.'

Suddenly and without warning, his arms were round her, his mouth roughly pressed against hers. Elaine relaxed, her body leaned against his, her mouth eager for his kisses, her happiness for that moment almost too wonderful to bear.

And then she remembered Felicity. If Garvin told her how Elaine had kissed him and clung to him, how Felicity would laugh and say 'Poor Elaine, she has nothing in life.' And probably think, 'I have every-thing.'

Elaine knew Garvin was not kissing her because he loved her—but it was a sort of masculine joke. She pushed him away. 'Don't!'

'And why not? I'm not murdering you! What's wrong with a man kissing a girl?'

'What would Marge say?' Elaine asked, and wondered why she hadn't said Felicity. Was it, perhaps, the fear that Garvin might admit that he and Felicity were going to marry?

'Marge?' Garvin sounded puzzled. 'Oh, Marge! What would she say? Probably that she wished I was kissing her.'

'Why aren't you?'

He began to laugh and let go of her. Immediately she wished she had gone on standing still in the close warmth of his arms.

'Marge?' Garvin asked again. 'Haven't you met her? She lives on the other side of the island. Her father is an ornithologist. An only daughter, she's often lonely, because her mother is dead. She goes to the same school as the girls.'

'School?' Elaine gasped. 'Is she still at school?'

'Yes. She's fifteen or so. These days at that age they reckon they're grown up. She's a nice kid. She loves to fuss—that's why she looks after my hideout.' He chuckled. 'Imagine me kissing Marge! If I did, it would just be a peck on the cheek, because I wouldn't want her to think the kiss meant anything.'

Elaine looked at him, or at least what she could see, for he was a dark silhouette against the star-splashed sky and she couldn't see his face or expression. He hadn't given her a peck on the cheek.

'Seriously, Elaine,' Garvin's voice was grave, 'you've been a great help to my family and I do appreciate it. Not only Tommy but Aunt Rosemary as well. It hadn't struck me that I was hindering your progress as a professional dancer and that perhaps the big chance of your life lies in the hands of Mike who's waiting for you in England.'

'He isn't!'

'Felicity says he is. She should know.'

Fury swept through Elaine so that it was hard to speak, but she managed to say: 'I don't care what Felicity says. She makes it all up. I know Mike and that he'll never forgive me for turning down that audition. He says it made him look a fool, as if he'd wasted their time, choosing the wrong kind of girl. On the ship he made it plain that he has no interest in me or my work, because he hardly spoke to me.'

'Maybe he changed his mind after you left the ship?'

'I didn't leave the ship, I was taken from it!' Elaine almost shouted.

Garvin chuckled. 'Touché! So I've been wasting your time—valuable at your age, because you may be missing opportunities to make your dreams come true. You want to tour the world, don't you? Particularly America. I didn't realise how you were longing to go back, but now I do, I've arranged everything. I've made a booking for you to fly to London, tomorrow.'

It was like a smack in the face to Elaine. 'Tomorrow?' she gasped.

'Yes. I'll take you to the mainland and see you on the plane. Your mother will be glad to see you.'

And you'll be glad to see me go—and so will Felicity, Elaine was thinking, still too dazed to grasp it all. Tomorrow?

How pleased Felicity would be. Once again she had won. Not that there was ever any question of Elaine winning—but there had been that small lifeless hope.

Tomorrow. Garvin would see her on the plane and never would she see him again.

Never. Never.

CHAPTER TWELVE

As Elaine found her voice, she pretended to yawn and said: 'I'm sleepy. I think I'll go to bed.'

But Garvin's hand was on her arm. 'Oh no, you're not. Your last night with us?'

So back into the crowd they went. Everyone congratulated her on the dancing, but what riled her was the look on Felicity's face and the way her eyes were triumphant. Crowing with delight, Elaine thought miserably, but she made herself laugh and talk as if it was what she wanted to do—go home.

Lady Rosemary said they would miss Elaine but that she quite understood the importance of Elaine's career. 'You are, as Felicity says, an ambitious girl, and quite right, too, my dear. You're a fine dancer.'

Emily and Patricia had plenty of questions to ask about what it was like to be a professional dancer. 'Will you get world-famous?' Emily wanted to know.

Garvin smiled. 'Elaine will get what's she's after. She's independent and ambitious. She can't lose.'

It was all Elaine could manage to do to laugh with them. She couldn't lose? Well, what was she doing now? She had lost the man she loved—though could she really say that, for

131

don't you have to own something before you lose it?

Elaine was dancing when she realised she hadn't seen Garvin for some time. She looked round the ballroom which was no longer so crowded and saw that Felicity wasn't there either. They were together. Garvin could not even spare Elaine her last evening.

Somehow Elaine managed to slip away, first saying goodnight to Lady Rosemary, who was sympathetic.

'Yes, my dear girl, you must be tired. You used a lot of energy in that dancing. You did enjoy the party?'

'Very much indeed,' Elaine lied. 'It's been a wonderful party.'

'I'm glad you liked it, dear.'

Something Elaine had wondered came to her mind. 'Is this island's name really Paradise Island?' she asked.

Lady Rosemary laughed. 'No, my dear girl, it isn't. Its real name is Mepita Island, but when my husband brought me here after our honeymoon, I said it was Paradise, and I've called it that ever since. I was fortunate in having a very happy marriage and have enjoyed my life here. Even now, old as I am, I am fortunate enough to have my grandchildren to love and to love me. This is indeed Paradise.'

It was . . . or it would be, Elaine thought miserably, if only . . .

She realised tears were near, so she hurriedly kissed the old lady goodnight and fled to her bedroom where there was no one to see her weakness. It took ages before she found sanctuary in sleep, for the words in her mind went on and on, like someone relentlessly banging a drum.

Redundant—so off you go! Your last evening. Farewell for ever.

Luckily she woke early, as she had to pack her clothes. She went down to breakfast and found Lady Rosemary looking worried.

'It's so unlike Garvin,' she said. 'He must be feeling very ill if he admits it.'

'Garvin—ill?' Elaine said quickly, then wished she hadn't said it in such a shocked voice, for surely it would give away her secret?

Felicity had noticed, for she was smiling. 'He's probably got 'flu.'

'No, it's worse than that,' Lady Rosemary said. 'He's feverish, sweating terribly. I've sent for the doctor.'

Looking at her wrist watch, Felicity said to Elaine, 'The car will be round in an hour. I hope you've packed and are ready to go.'

Elaine stared at her. There was so much she wanted to say and could have said, yet how could she upset the kindly old lady who had enough to worry her as it was, without being involved in two girls fighting. Elaine's hand itched to hit that smug, pompous, triumphant face that was looking at her with amusement.

'I'm quite ready,' she said quietly.

But how could she go when Garvin was so ill? How could she leave him—go thousands of miles away, never to see him again, perhaps never to hear if he was still ill . . . How could she go?

But what else could she do? She could hardly say she would not go, because there was no reason why she should demand to stay. Garvin was no relation . . . he was only the man she loved so much, but no one must know, if she could help it. Of course Felicity knew, but that couldn't be helped.

The hour hurried by with Lady Rosemary pacing up and down worriedly wondering why the doctor was taking so long to get there. She had been to see Garvin several times and he was no better.

Elaine went up to her room and hesitated outside Garvin's bedroom door. Could she go in? Would she be welcome or would he be annoyed?

It so happened that Pierre, the butler, came along with a tray of long glasses with cold drinks. He gave a funny little bow, opened the door and stood back, gesturing to Elaine to go in before him. So in she went.

Garvin was in bed, covered only by a sheet, and the perspiration was pouring down his red face as he twisted and turned uncomfortably.

'Garvin,' Elaine said gently. 'How are you?'

He looked at her through half-closed eyes.

'Feeling like hell warmed up,' he said irritably, 'and not in the mood for visitors.'

'I came to say good-bye.'

'Good-bye, then,' he grumbled, and turned again, wiping his hand over his face.

Pierre put the tray on the table by Garvin's side, touched Elaine's arm gently and pointed at the door, so she followed him and stood in the corridor as he closed the door.

'The Master is not good when ill,' Pierre said with a smile. 'You must forgive.'

Elaine had to smile. 'He is forgiven. Is he very bad?'

Pierre shrugged his shoulders. 'I think it is bad, but the doctor will say. Your luggage is in the hall and the car has come.'

'Thank you, Pierre,' said Elaine.

She had dressed for the journey in a lilac-coloured linen suit and white blouse. From her room, she took her shoulder bag and made certain she had left nothing and then went down the stairs.

Felicity was there, frowning. 'The car is waiting,' she said impatiently.

Lady Rosemary came up from the terrace. 'That doctor,' she said worriedly. 'I'll have a few things to say to him when he gets here. You going now, Elaine dear? I am sorry. We shall miss you, but we mustn't be selfish. You must think of your future. Your work must come first.'

'I'm sorry, too.' Elaine said, uncomfortably

conscious of Felicity's smug smile. 'Do you think Garvin will be all right?'

'Of course he will. These tropical fevers always look worse than they are,' Felicity said impatiently.

'This is a bad one,' Lady Rosemary told her, her voice gently reprimanding. 'If only the doctor would come! You must come again, Elaine dear. Garvin has your address?'

'I . . . I think so.'

'Look, we must go, Elaine. You'll miss the plane,' said Felicity.

'I can go alone. There's no need for you to come,' Elaine said quickly. Imagine putting up with Felicity for an hour and a half at least! An unbearable thought.

Felicity laughed. 'Garvin said I was to make sure you caught the plane.'

In other words, Elaine interpreted, it was to make sure Elaine goes!

'Don't worry, I'll go,' she snapped, her good intentions vanishing. 'I'll go alone.'

She saw the puzzled look on the old lady's face and realised how rude she must have sounded, but she could stand no more and brushed past Felicity, looking back to wave good-bye to the silent Lady Rosemary.

The car was waiting, but on the steps was a tall man with a bald head and very blue eyes.

'Doctor . . . at last!' Lady Rosemary exclaimed, hurrying to meet him. 'Garvin is very sick. High temperature, pain, sweating like mad . . .'

The doctor was frowning, looking at Elaine. 'Where are you going?' he asked.

Felicity came outside. 'We're going to the airport. She's on her way home to England.'

The doctor frowned. 'I'm afraid she can't go until I know what's wrong with Garvin. There have been a few cholera cases lately and we've been warned to watch out for symptoms.'

'But she's booked to go,' Felicity said.

'I'm sorry, but you'd better cancel it,' the doctor retorted. 'She'll have to stay until I know for sure what's wrong. Meanwhile you're all in quarantine and must stay in the house.'

'You think it's cholera, Dr. Mackenzie?' Lady Rosemary sounded horrified.

He smiled. 'No, I don't think it is for a moment, but I can't allow this young lady to go on a crowded plane and perhaps pass on the virus to dozens of people.' He turned to Elaine. 'I'm sorry to have to do this, but you can't go until I'm sure.'

'When will you be sure?' Felicity demanded.

He shrugged. 'How can I say until I've seen the patient?' He went up the stairs with Lady Rosemary. Felicity shouted at the chauffeur to bring in the luggage, then looked at Elaine.

'Well, you'll have to put up with us for a little longer.'

'I'll have to cancel the flight bookings,' said Elaine, dazed for the moment. Could Garvin be so ill? Just how dangerous was cholera?

'I'll do it for you,' Felicity said crossly. 'What a blessed nuisance! Goodness knows when you'll get another booking. They're pretty busy.' She went to the library where the telephone was.

Elaine walked down the hall to the terrace. She stood there, staring at the beautiful garden but seeing nothing. All she could think of was Garvin upstairs with the doctor examining him. Just how bad was cholera? If only she knew . . . she had heard of terrible epidemics of cholera, but did it always mean . . .

A terrible feeling of sickness swept through her and suddenly her legs felt weak, so she sat down. Fortunately there was a chair handy.

She heard Lady Rosemary talking in the hall some half an hour later. The old lady looked relieved when she came out.

'It's not cholera, dear, but he doesn't know what it is. It may be anything, and he says you must not go home for a few days. He's taking some specimens of Garvin's blood and urine and hopes to know before long just what is wrong.' She sighed. 'I'm afraid Garvin is in a very bad temper and says the doctor has no right to keep you from going home as it might ruin your opportunities.'

So Garvin did want her to go, Elaine thought as she smiled at the old lady. 'I'm in no hurry, Lady Rosemary. Mother has several of us dancers, so I'm not really needed. I'm sorry Garvin is so ill, but . . .'

Felicity came out. 'I rang up and cancelled everything. I'm going up to see Garvin.'

'I shouldn't,' Lady Rosemary said with a smile. 'He's in a bad temper, and also the injection the doctor gave him will make him sleepy.'

'I'm used to his temper, and he's rarely cross with me,' Felicity said with a smile and turned back into the house.

'Then you don't mind the delay, my dear?' Lady Rosemary said to Elaine as Pierre brought out cold drinks.

'No.'

'But your career? Isn't it terribly important to you? I mean, I thought you were very ambitious.'

'I was, but now I'm not so sure,' Elaine confessed truthfully. 'My career was important to me, but somehow it doesn't seem so important any more.'

'I wonder why you've changed?' Lady Rosemary mused.

Elaine shrugged. 'I honestly don't know. Perhaps because I've found other things just as—or even more—important.'

Lady Rosemary nodded. 'Maybe at home you have your mother always talking about dancing and your possible future. I know a lot of mothers are like that.'

Nodding, Elaine said: 'Yes, my mother was

very ambitious when young. Unfortunately she got injured on the stage when something fell on her foot and she couldn't dance any more, so she had to take up teaching the dancing she loved so much. It must have been hard on her.'

'Very, and she's trying to replace her loss by having a daughter who can take her place? When you do, it will help her a lot.'

'I hadn't thought of it like that,' Elaine admitted.

The old lady gently touched Elaine's hand. 'There are many things we don't think of until we grow old, my dear girl. I'm sure you're going to make your mother very happy. That reminds me,' she said, getting up, 'the doctor wants the children to come home from school and not go back until he knows what's wrong with Garvin. I must ring the headmistress and then send the car.'

*   *   *

It was a whole week before the doctor allowed the children to return to school and Elaine to fly home—a miserable week for Elaine. She felt confused, because she seemed to be torn in two. Part of her was glad she could stay on until Garvin was well—but the other part suffered, for Felicity kept saying he didn't want any visitors, except her and the old lady. Elaine felt so near him and yet so far. It was slow torture, and many a night her pillow was wet from her tears.

Maybe it would be better when she had gone and was far away. But mightn't it be worse, for here there was a chance that he might suddenly get well and come downstairs where she could see him?

But he didn't want to see her . . . That was obvious.

The car came for her. Lady Rosemary kissed her warmly.

'You must come again, my dear. You simply must,' she said.

Felicity looked amused. 'That'll be the day,' she said, too quietly for the old lady, who was slightly deaf, to hear but loud enough to be sure Elaine heard! 'Garvin will feel much better once you're gone,' Felicity added, still as quietly.

Elaine smiled sweetly. 'I'm sure he will, with you to look after him . . . and lie,' she added, almost whispering the words, following Felicity's method.

Elaine ran down to the car and told the chauffeur to drive fast to the airport. The sooner she was away the better.

Once out of sight of the house, she put her hands to her eyes and fought back the tears. But how could she help but cry when she knew she would never see Garvin again?

CHAPTER THIRTEEN

It was a long tiring journey in which everything that could go wrong did. First they had a puncture before they reached the island airport, so there was a bit of a panic on the part of the chauffeur as he hastily changed the tyre. Then once there, an hour to wait! They flew to the mainland and had another three hours to wait. Finally the flight back to Heathrow, and something went wrong as they arrived and the plane circled three or four times before landing. Then the usual irritating fight to find your luggage as it rumbled by on the moving panel and then waiting for the bus to Victoria. By then, Elaine was so tired and cold as well as miserable that she took a taxi to her mother's home in Kensington.

She let herself in with her key and her mother came out of the kitchen. 'Elaine darling! It can't be you . . . I had no idea. Oh, how lovely—and just when I had some good news for you,' her mother said as she hugged her. 'You look dead tired. Come and have a cup of tea. I'm only just back from the school. Why didn't you let me know you were coming?'

Elaine smiled ruefully. 'It's a long story, Mum. Can I flop for a bit?'

'Of course. Look, go and have a quick bath,

142

don't bother to dress. I'll get us something to eat as well as drink.' The tall slim woman with elegantly curled honey-brown hair had only the slightest limp to give evidence of the tragedy when her future as a dancer was lost.

Elaine found it pleasant to lie in the hot water, to rub herself dry and put on her nightie and dressing-gown, then went downstairs to the pleasantly warm large kitchen where they always ate.

'Sit down, dear, you're looking really tired. What happened? You didn't tell me much in your letter, you know. Why did you leave the ship? And why wasn't Dirk your partner? You didn't give me your address when you wrote, so I couldn't answer,' Lily Thomas said as she moved round the kitchen, putting a tray in front of Elaine. 'There's so much I just couldn't understand.'

Elaine smiled. 'As I said, it's a long story, but the bath did me good. It's just been a bad day with everything going wrong, but it's good to be home.'

Her mother smiled. 'It's good to have you, darling. Now start at the beginning. You liked it on the ship and you liked your partner. Why wasn't he Dirk?'

It was a long story, but Elaine tried to condense it as much as possible, yet her mother was still listening afterwards as they sat in the lounge before the electric heater. There was so much to tell: Elaine's surprise when she

143

found she had to dance with a stranger. What a good dancer he had proved to be and how she enjoyed it. 'Mike was on the ship, too.'

'Mike?' Her mother lifted her hand. 'I've some news for you from Mike—but carry on. I can tell you that later. What was he doing on the ship?'

'Chatting up Felicity.'

'Not *the* Felicity? Tommy's girl-friend? She was there too?'

'Yes, Mum.'

Then Elaine told her mother about the trip to see the island and Garvin's threat to keep her there until she had told him where Tommy was.

'He couldn't have meant it—Mr. Humfrey, I mean.' Elaine's mother sounded shocked.

'I don't know. There was I, standing on this lonely beach with not a man or animal in sight and there was the liner going out to sea. I was frightened. It seems stupid, looking back, but at the time . . .' Then she told her mother about the breakfast he had cooked, the car fetching them, her shock when she saw her luggage, the amazement she felt as they saw the other side of the island and met Lady Rosemary.

'It was heartbreaking, Mum. When Garvin told her he hadn't found out where Tommy was, her face just wrinkled up with shock and the tears fell. So did mine. I'd have given anything to help them find Tommy.'

'What about Tommy's girl-friend? Didn't she know?'

'Felicity? Well, if she did she didn't tell Garvin. Actually I don't think she did know. She hardly spoke to me, though I was at the same dining table. She and Mike went together when Felicity hadn't got Garvin.'

'So she was playing double-handed?'

'Yes, and succeeding. Garvin is crazy about her.'

Her mother looked at her sharply, recognising the note of despair, but decided her daughter was too tired to answer unwelcome questions.

'So you met Lady Rosemary and . . .'

'The two girls.' There was so much to tell her mother about Garvin and his six wards and his anxiety about Tommy, who had become so difficult.

'Lady Rosemary said it frightened her, because he seemed to . . . recede was her word, just sit and stare into space. She was full of praise for Garvin who, she said, did his very best to help Tommy.'

'And then? I mean, why did you stay on with them if you knew nothing about Tommy. Oh, and the ship? What about the dancing?'

'Garvin told me he had arranged for Dirk to fly out with a partner.'

'Is that so?' Mrs. Thomas nodded. 'I haven't seen Dirk for some time. Usually he's around. Maybe he will be now you're home.' She

145

smiled at Elaine, having always told her that Dirk would make a good husband. 'So? Go on. I'm fascinated.'

So Elaine told her about Felicity's arrival— and then how Tommy had walked in with his wife.

'It was amazing to see the difference in him. The responsibility is already doing him good. They're both teaching.'

'Tommy teaching? I can't imagine.'

'Teaching art. He'll have time to do his own painting, and Jackie is just . . .'

'His cup of tea? How did the grandmother and Mr. Humfrey react?'

'Both liked Jackie, and were ever so pleased. They made a lovely couple.'

Again there was a wistful note in Elaine's voice and it was all her mother could do not to ask questions. 'And then?'

'Well, they gave a party and . . .' Elaine noticed to her dismay that her voice wasn't steady.

'And you got hurt?' her mother said very quietly.

Elaine looked at her. 'He didn't mean to hurt me, but . . . but he had asked me to stay and keep his aunt, but once Tommy was all right, I'd said I wasn't needed and he said . . . he said when I was redundant he would tell me.'

'Redundant? That's a funny word to use.'

'It's a horrible word.' Elaine shivered. 'Then . .

. then Lady Rosemary gave the party and . . . well, Garvin said he was being selfish in keeping me away from home when such a good opportunity was available. I didn't know what he was talking about, but he said Felicity had said he was stopping my ambitions from coming true . . . My ambitions,' Elaine said bitterly, turning away, hoping her mother had not seen the tears in her eyes.

'So?' her mother said gently.

'Garvin said I was booked to go the next day. It was an awful shock, and . . . and then he was ill, some tropical fever, but the doctor wouldn't let me go in case it was cholera or something infectious, so I had to wait another week.'

'You didn't mind?' her mother asked quietly.

Elaine looked up, her eyes wide with misery. 'I did and I didn't. Garvin was so ill, but he refused to see me. He only saw Lady Rosemary and Felicity. He . . . he wouldn't see me even to say good-bye.'

'He sounds a most unpleasant person to me,' Mrs. Thomas commented. 'Selfish, arrogant, callous. Let's face it—isn't he?'

'He doesn't mean to be . . .'

'You mean, you *hope* he doesn't mean to be. You've got it badly, my poor Elaine. You can talk of no one but Garvin Humfrey. Thank goodness you have your dancing. That at least will help. Now we must concentrate on your

147

future. That reminds me, Mike rang up to ask when you'd be back. He's arranged an audition for you.'

'He has?' Elaine sat up, startled. 'It can't be true!'

Her mother smiled. 'Why can't it be? I mean, after all, he took the trouble to phone me and ask if you would contact him as soon as you return. I gather it's a rather wonderful chance on television.' Her voice changed: 'You don't believe me?'

Elaine looked round the cosy modern room with its bright colours and trendy furniture. So very different from Lady Rosemary's Paradise.

'Of course I believe you, Mum, but . . . Look, I thought Felicity was lying. I mean, she told Garvin that Mike had said I promised to go to an audition on my return, but I never did, because he never asked me.'

'Well, he seems to think this is a big chance. You will ring him?'

Hesitating, Elaine looked at her mother's anxious face. It couldn't be true, it just couldn't be, but . . . It meant so much to her mother. 'Even though it means nothing to me,' Elaine thought, remembering what Lady Rosemary had said.

'Yes, of course I will,' she promised.

Her mother's face brightened. 'That's the best cure for a broken heart, darling. You get a good chance on television and who knows where it may lead to. It was foolish of you to

148

let yourself fall in love with such a man as Garvin Humfrey—wealthy, obviously a rich girl's dream, for they usually want more than they've got. It seems he behaved very oddly.'

'He's a wonderful dancer. Quite the best.'

'That doesn't make him a good husband, darling,' her mother said with a laugh.

'Oh, I knew from the beginning that he . . . well, he liked dancing with me, but that was all. Otherwise he just didn't *see* me.'

'Then don't see him. He's not worth breaking your heart over. Now if it had been Dirk . . . I thought you and he . . .'

Elaine laughed, a weak caricature of her usual laughter, her mother noticed. 'I did think at one time that Dirk . . .'

'He'd make a good husband. Two good, ambitious dancers. What could be better? You did *think,* you admit? So this is the second time you have *thought*—you obviously don't know. One day you'll meet someone and you'll know, darling. I know it's not going to be easy. I loved someone who jilted me before I met your father, so I know what it's like. Absolute hell. Let's be glad you've got your dancing. Forget men and concentrate on your future.'

Elaine smiled weakly. Bless her, Mum was doing her best to help, but how could anyone, no matter how hurt they might have been in the past, know the agony of it all? She thought of Garvin still in bed, Felicity by his side, stroking his hand, holding it against her cheek

149

and Garvin smiling at her . . . Something seemed to choke her, so she stood up.

'Mind if I go to bed, Mum? I'm really . . .'

Her mother stood up. 'I know, darling. Look, I promised to look in for a chat with old Mrs. Yelton. Will you be all right if I go?'

Elaine laughed. 'Of course, Mum. No nonsense like committing suicide. I'm so tired I'll soon sleep. I'll ring Mike tomorrow. Goodnight.'

'Goodnight, darling,' her mother said, looking sad as she wished there was more she could do. But this was something Elaine had to fight alone.

The next few days were a sort of controlled nightmare for Elaine. She could not stop thinking about Garvin, wondering if he was better, wishing she could find out. It was so absurd, but she hadn't their address, all she knew was the name of the island—but was that enough? If only she knew!

Her mother had said that first morning at breakfast, 'I must ring our agent today to let him know you're available, darling. You won't go back to your job at once, will you?'

Elaine sighed. 'No, Mum.' She didn't want to go anywhere—except back to Paradise Island.

'Good, because you'd better wait and see Mike. If it's to do with the television thing, you'll need to be free all day. I can't wait for you to have the audition. I'm sure Mike must feel you've a good chance or he wouldn't bother. Aren't you thrilled? I know I would be.'

Smiling, Elaine tried to look enthusiastic. The truth was she didn't know *what* to do—she was drifting in fog with no directions. She just wanted to curl up and hug herself and try not to cry. She was so sure that at the beginning, on the ship, Garvin *had* liked her. Both had enjoyed their dancing and their talks. It was when Felicity took over, so beautiful, so witty, so . . . such a liar! Or was she? Elaine wondered. Had she misjudged Felicity? If Mike really had arranged an audition?

So she phoned Mike. 'So you're back at last,' he said, his voice disapproving. 'Where have you been all this time?'

'On the island.'

'What island? Oh yes, I know,' Mike said quickly. 'Well, you've left it a bit late. I'll have to get to work and see about it.'

'Could we meet? I hate discussing things on the phone.'

'Meet?' said Mike, sounding a bit confused. 'Well . . .'

'You haven't heard if Garvin is all right?'

'Yes, he's up and about, but still rather weak. Why? Interested?'

'He wasn't at all well when I left, Mike. He wouldn't see anyone but Lady Rosemary and Felicity.'

'She's still there,' Mike told her. 'Think

151

they're going to marry?' he asked.

It was like the thrust of a sword. 'I . . . think so, don't you?'

'I don't know. I know she's pretty keen, but I didn't think it had got that close.' Mike sounded annoyed.

'She seems to think so.'

'And you?'

Elaine drew a deep breath. How it hurt to discuss it all so casually! 'He seems infatuated.'

'Oh, does he? Look, Elaine, come and have lunch with me in four days and I'll have some news for you.'

'Thanks, Mike.'

She rang off and stood staring at the phone for a few moments. Had he really the chance of a job for her? Or was it all a contrived lie?

Her mother was doing her best to help Elaine forget —as if that was ever possible! There were several schools where Elaine's mother went to teach dancing and now, claiming a cold, she got Elaine to take her place. It kept Elaine busy, but it didn't stop her memory.

At the next monthly dance held at a Kensington hotel, Dirk turned up.

'Hi,' he said, just as tall and dark and handsome as ever. 'Long time no see. I want to talk to you, young woman. What was behind all this business?'

He took her to the bar, got them drinks and found a quiet table. Elaine told him. 'And I thought you were to be my partner, Dirk. I had the shock of my life when this stranger turned up. Why weren't you there?'

'I was on holiday, as you know, but planned to come back, then I got a cable from my agent saying I wasn't needed so soon. I was furious when I found myself landed with Anne Pettigan as a partner. A nice kid but no dancer. She did her best but spent most of her time flirting with the old men.' He laughed. 'It would have been so different had you been there. I've missed you. What made you go on that island?'

'They thought I could help them find Tommy.'

'I saw him the other day. He's married. She's quite a dish.'

'We all liked her. They'll be going down to Cornwall to their new jobs.'

'Funny to think of young Tommy as a husband and maybe, one day, a father. I'd never have thought he'd do it. How do you feel about marriage, Elaine? Is that stupid bit of paper and some stuttering nervous-said words really necessary? I mean, it all seems such a waste of time, and as for the white weddings and all that money thrown away,' he said scornfully. 'A lot of tripe. Look, come and dance.'

It was pleasant to dance with Dirk again— yet at the same time it hurt, for she found herself wishing she was in Garvin's arms all the time. She made herself laugh and talk and hoped Dirk would not guess the truth—that her feeling for him might have been affection, friendship, talking the same language, but it had never been love.

She knew that now. Now that she knew what love really was.

'I'll drive you home,' Dirk said at the end of the evening. 'Your mother said she won't be back for nearly an hour as she's going out for a drink with her latest boy-friend. Have you met him? Nice bloke, bit of a square. Widower. Believes you should wait a year before you choose another woman. What a waste of time!'

'You think Mum is going to marry him? She hasn't said anything.'

Dirk laughed. 'Neither has he. He's still got three months to go, but they get on like a house on fire. Everyone knows. A good thing, too, your mother's had a hard battle.'

He drove Elaine along the always busy streets of Kensington to the small terrace house that was her home.

'What about a drink—one for the road?' he said. 'Your mother told me she has my favourite beer.'

'Of course,' Elaine said wearily.

Once inside, she got the bottles and glasses and went to sit down, but Dirk moved fast. In a moment, he was sitting on the couch, with Elaine sprawled over his knees as his mouth met hers, rough, demanding and . . .

Disgusting! Elaine realised it at once, and she put both her hands on his chest and pushed him away. 'Don't do that!' she shouted. 'Don't!'

He let go of her so that she rolled off his lap on to the floor, luckily carpeted. 'Why not?' he asked. 'You never objected before.'

She stood up slowly. 'Before isn't now,' she said.

He stood up, too, and frowned. 'What does that mean? That there's someone else?'

She turned away, her hands hiding her eyes. 'I'm terribly sorry, Dirk. I thought it was you until . . . until I met him. And then I knew that what I felt for you wasn't love.' She lowered her hands and looked at him through a tearful daze. 'I like you so much, Dirk, we've had some pleasant times together, but that isn't love.'

'What is love?' he asked roughly. 'Is this because I said I wasn't impressed by marriage? Is that what you want?'

'Yes, I do, but . . . but not from you.'

'Why not?'

'Because I don't love you. I am sorry, Dirk. I know how I feel, so I can understand how you must.'

'What do you mean? How you feel? Isn't he going to marry you?'

'He doesn't even see me,' she said, her voice like a wail. 'I'm sorry, Dirk, I . . .'

'He must be mad or blind. Well, if you change your mind, give me a ring,' Dirk said curtly, and left the house.

Alone, Elaine really cried. It didn't help things, but neither could she stop the tears. What was she to do with her life? She no longer enjoyed dancing, her ambitions had vanished, and now her mother was in love with a nice widower. This Elaine was glad about, for her mother was lonely and if he was a nice man—as according to Dirk he was—then . . .

She ran up to her bedroom, undressed and jumped into bed. She would pretend to be asleep when her mother came home, for she just could not answer any questions that night.

Yet sleep would not come, for the questions went round and round in her mind, like a crazy toy. What should she do with her life? Unwanted.

Or as Garvin would say: *Redundant.*

CHAPTER FOURTEEN

Elaine went to lunch with Mike rather sure that there would be no audition at all—that he had just made it all up. On the other hand, her mother believed him and was very keen about it.

They ate lunch, talking casually of the island, what it was like and had she seen

Tommy and his little wife. It wasn't until the coffee came that Elaine looked at him and said:

'There isn't going to be an audition, is there, Mike?'

He looked startled. 'What made you say that?'

'I know you, Mike. You're on edge as if you're not sure what to say. Besides, if there was one, I don't want it.'

'You don't? I mean, wouldn't?' He sounded surprised.

'Look, Mike, I believe this is all Felicity's doing,' Elaine said firmly.

He looked uncomfortable and round the restaurant as if afraid their conversation would be overheard. 'To be honest with you, there wasn't a second audition. There was the first.'

'I know, and I'm sorry I had to miss it, but the other job was definite, whereas the audition might have had no result. So it was Felicity's idea? But why?'

He smiled. 'You must be blind. She fancies Garvin and wanted you out of the way.'

'That wasn't necessary,' Elaine said bitterly.

He lifted his eyebrows. 'Don't be daft. On the ship, he quite fell for you—that was why Felicity chased him and then made out you were ambition-mad, so must be allowed to go back to England. She wrote and told me all about it—seemed to think she was clever. She's playing us both—Garvin and me. He's the one with money, but I think it's me she loves. Unfortunately money means so much to her.'

'I thought she was rich.'

'She is—but it's often the rich women who want more, and she does. I was chatting her up because her father owns several theatres and I'm resting at the moment. Things are rather tough, so I thought if I got to know her well—I mean, I'd met her at your mother's dance, but that was all. Then when I heard she was going on the ship because she knew Garvin was going, I managed to get a cancellation, too. By the way, I hear Garvin has bought several theatres, so maybe he'd help me out.'

'I'm sure he would. You're a good actor, Mike.'

He smiled. 'Thanks. I wish I could convince them. I think we're mad to be actors. You never can be sure.'

'I think that applies to nearly everything, Mike. Well, thanks for the lunch.'

'I'm sorry about the other. It was mean of me.'

Elaine smiled. 'That's all right. It's amazing what Felicity can do.'

Catching a bus in the crowded Knightsbridge Elaine thought: 'Well, at least that's off.' She knew now she never wanted to dance again. After the joy and wonder of dancing with Garvin, she hated the thought of dancing with anyone else. Yet if she told her mother that . . . all the years of work wasted, such talent ignored, her mother would say, and be bitterly hurt.

Suppose she went back to her job? Elaine thought. She could still do odd jobs of dancing. A secretary was always wanted, or she could go back to her old job, they had told her so. She felt absurdly tired, so she decided to leave that until the next day.

That evening, her mother came into the house and called excitedly:

'Elaine . . . Elaine . . . some wonderful news!'

Elaine came from the kitchen where she had been preparing the dinner. 'What's so wonderful, Mum?'

Her mother could hardly speak for a moment. 'I can't get over it, darling. It's your dream come true!'

For a moment Elaine thought that meant Garvin had come to see her—and to tell her he loved her. But the next moment she knew it could not be that, for her mother went on:

'Our agent phoned me—a wonderful chance. A dance tour of Europe and America!'

'For me? Alone?'

Her mother shook her head. 'Oh no. You'll have a partner. He's coming to see you tomorrow. He says you must dance together before any contract is signed. Oh, Elaine, it will do you so much good, bring back the colour in your cheeks and the sparkle in your eye. How did you get on with Mike? Is this going to clash?'

Elaine smiled. 'I was right, Mum. There isn't a second audition.'

'Then why did he ring me?'

'It was Felicity's doing. To get me out of the way, Mike said.'

'He told you? He must feel ashamed.'

'I think he does. He was very apologetic.'

'Anyhow, darling, this man is coming tomorrow to our school. So you will be there at eleven o'clock, won't you? Wear one of your prettiest dresses, because your appearance is important, too. Oh, Elaine love,' her mother was twisting her hands just as Elaine did when worried or excited, 'this might be your great chance. Who knows who's going to see you? You've always wanted to dance in America, haven't you?'

'Yes, I have,' Elaine managed to say. She hadn't the heart to tell her mother the truth now—that dancing was out, where possible. If she couldn't dance with Garvin, she didn't want to dance at all! However, this opportunity if turned down would disappoint her mother so much. 'I won't be late, I promise,' she said.

It was with mixed feelings that she took her lovely white satin dress with her next morning. She could change in the school. She did, keeping an eye on her watch and going to the main room at exactly eleven o'clock.

They would have the school to themselves, for her mother had gone down to Surbiton to give lessons at a new boarding school, and there were no private lessons dated for the morning. As Elaine opened the door of the big main room, she tried to relax her tense muscles and make herself smile. A man was standing by the window, looking at the window-box of red geraniums. He turned round and Elaine stopped dead, her hand flying to her mouth.

'Why, it's you!' she gasped.

Garvin smiled. 'And why not? I thought we would both enjoy a dancing tour of Europe and America, so it's all arranged if you'll be my partner.'

'You must be joking,' Elaine said slowly.

'Why should I be joking? We both need a holiday and we both enjoy dancing. So that makes sense.'

'But . . . but . . .' She couldn't speak properly It couldn't be true? A tour of the world with Garvin as her partner? But how could she bear it, loving him as she did? 'But what about Felicity?'

He came slowly towards her. 'What about Felicity?'

'Well . . . well . . . aren't you going to marry her?'

Garvin's eyebrows nearly met. 'Good grief, the nonsense you talk sometimes! First you suggested I should be kissing a fifteen-year-old schoolgirl and now you're trying to marry me off to Felicity. What put that in your mind?'

He was standing very near her now. Elaine clenched her hands tightly behind her back and tried to keep her voice light. 'Felicity did. You wouldn't see anyone when you were ill except Lady Rosemary and Felicity.'

'That's not true. I was hurt because you never bothered to come.'

'I came once and you told me to get out.'

'I remember. I felt terrible. I apologise.' He smiled. 'But the other times I never said only Aunt Rosemary or Felicity.'

'Well, that's what she told me. Also . . . also it was obvious to anyone that you were in love with her.'

'You think I loved Felicity? You must be mad! Now look, Elaine, will you come round the world with me, or not? We'll have a lot of fun, and it'll be a new kind of honeymoon.'

She stared at him. 'What did you say?' she asked, her eyes wide with amazement.

Garvin smiled. 'You heard me all right.' He put his hand on her bare arm and she shivered. The next second she was in his arms, his mouth hard against hers. Then he let her go, still holding her, but not so close.

'Listen, Elaine. Let's get this clear. I was never in love with Felicity. If I seemed to be chatting her up it was a foolish attempt on my part to make you jealous.'

She smiled. 'You succeeded! I was jealous of

Marge and Felicity.'

'You didn't show it. Know something, darling? You're a funny girl—always so tense, so wary, looking at me as if afraid of what I'm going to do next. We were so close on the ship and then we seemed to drift apart. I couldn't understand it until Felicity pointed out that you were ambitious and didn't want to give up your profession. I wondered if that was why you never encouraged me. You never let me know if you loved me or not.'

'But how could I? You . . . you just didn't seem to notice me.'

'The way you went off from the island, so eager to get back to London and your work— that hurt me. It was only when Aunt Rosemary told me I was an idiot and that it was obvious to any fool that you loved me—and then I thought I'd come and ask you. Then I thought of something else. You've always been ambitious, so perhaps we should help you achieve your aim and that then, afterwards, perhaps you would be content to settle down and be my wife.'

'Garvin, since I've known you, I've stopped being ambitious. I don't mind if I never dance again, so long as I dance with you. All I want is for you to love me and I don't mind where I go, but I must go with you.'

She was close in his arms again and as he kissed her, he said quietly: 'We love one another, that's all that matters.'

163